"It's going to be all right, Monique."

He felt her shoulders heave and thought she'd pull away. Like all the other times. But she didn't. She leaned into him, and placed her arms around his waist. He pulled her closer to him and began rubbing his hand across her back. "It's okay, sweetheart. You can let go. We're all very concerned. Everything is going to be all right." He brushed his lips across her temple and kissed her there.

She stilled. Her arms around him loosened slightly. Niko silently chided himself. He hadn't meant to kiss her. It was a reflex, pure and simple. She pulled back. He lifted his head, ready to apologize. Until he saw the look in her eyes, and how they quickly shifted from looking into his eyes to looking at his lips. Just before she leaned in and joined hers to them. She did this, but moved no further. So Niko took over. He slowly moved his head, rubbing his lips across hers, creating a delicious friction that immediately increased the heat. Her mouth opened, and it took all of his restraint not to plunder her sweetness like a love-starved youth. But she didn't need that type of treatment right now. She needed gentleness and kindness and understanding. He was there to give it all.

Books by Zuri Day

Harlequin Kimani Romance

Diamond Dreams
Champagne Kisses
Platinum Promises
Solid Gold Seduction
Secret Silver Nights

ZURI DAY

snuck her first Harlequin romance at the age of twelve from her older sister's off-limits collection and was hooked from page one. Knights in shining armor and happily-ever-afters filled her teen years and spurred a lifelong love of reading. That she now creates these stories as a full-time, award-winning author is a dream come true! Splitting her time between the stunning Caribbean islands and Southern California, she's always busy writing her next novel, but Zuri makes time to connect with readers and meet with book clubs. Contact her via Facebook, www.facebook.com/haveazuriday, or at Zuri@ZuriDay.com.

SECRET SILVER
Nights

ZURI DAY

HARLEQUIN® KIMANI™ ROMANCE

Those hushed clandestine love affairs

Of which others are unaware

Makes lover's lives a sweet delight
of public days and secret nights!

Recycling programs
for this product may
not exist in your area.

ISBN-13: 978-0-373-86370-9

SECRET SILVER NIGHTS

For questions and comments about the quality of this book please contact us at CustomerService@Harlequin.com.

Printed in U.S.A.

Dear Reader,

Volunteering on the presidential campaign and then attending the historical 2009 inauguration in Washington, D.C., was an incredible experience, one of the more memorable of my life.

As it turns out, some of the Drakes were there, too!

Niko is particularly inspired, so much so that after a long talk with his grandfather Walter and his family he decides to test the waters of a political career by running for mayor of Paradise Cove. The politics there are on a much smaller scale, and Niko feels a win is already in the bag, until a formidable opponent shows up and makes the race interesting in more ways than one. Ooh…I love it when a confident man gets his cage rattled by a sexy surprise!

Niko's family rallies around him for support, including his sister, Teresa. Her story is next. In the meantime, I'd love to hear from you at zuriday.com.

One love!

Zuri

A huge shout-out and thank you to "Team Zuri"
and the Z-Nation!

Chapter 1

"Niko. Heads up, guy. We've got a problem."

Attorney Nicodemus "Niko" Drake barely glanced away from the speech he was tweaking as his campaign manager threw down the day's *Cove Chronicle* newspaper next to the iPad that had his attention. April had turned to May, but that hadn't stopped the rain. And that it was Saturday didn't deter this perpetual go-getter from showing up at the office or his loyal sidekick from following suit. On Monday, Niko was speaking at a dinner for the members of the chamber of commerce. He wanted to make sure that the speech was just right.

"Niko, did you hear me?"

"How could I not hear you, man?" He didn't look up. "Even this early, seven in the morning, your voice reverberates off the walls."

Bryce Clinton plopped into the seat behind a desk that was a mere six feet away from where Niko sat. "All right. Don't pay attention. But later today when you get blindsided, don't say I didn't warn you."

At six foot one and a lean one hundred and ninety-five pounds, Niko rarely felt he had to be warned about anything. So Bryce's comment got his attention. He reached over the iPad and picked up the paper. The headline caught him at once: Newest Mayoral Candidate Promises A New Day.

Hmm, interesting. So far there'd been only two other residents silly enough to not drop out of the race the moment he'd announced his candidacy. So who was this fool?

He unfolded the newspaper to read the article and was hit with his second surprise of the morning. The photo of said "fool." Someone he not only knew but had actually sparred with...and lost.

"Well, I'll be damned."

"He finally gets it," Bryce announced to an imaginary audience. Bryce was not only Niko's campaign manager but one of his best friends for the past twenty-plus years. Having grown up together in the tony Golden Gates neighborhood of their town, Paradise Cove, the two had lost contact during their college years. But after running into each other at one of the local restaurants and discovering that they'd both returned to their roots, they'd reconnected around eighteen holes and a couple of beers. Their friendship continued as though no time had been lost.

"So what are you going to try to do with this one?" Bryce asked, eyeing his laptop and flipping through a myriad of emails. "She's not from around here, so your name is likely not to have the same effect that it did on your previous rivals."

"I know her."

Bryce's head shot up. "Huh?"

"Mo is Monique. I would have never made the connection."

"'Mo is Monique'? You've lost me."

"Monique Slater," Niko continued. "Successful attorney who practices in Los Angeles, or used to. Steel fist in a velvet glove who takes no prisoners, who's known for chewing up prosecutors for breakfast and spitting out judges for lunch."

Bryce pushed away from his desk, turned toward Niko

and laced his hands behind his head. "How do you know her?"

Niko relaxed his position as well, stretching his long, muscular legs out in front of him, and picked up the newspaper again. "I debated her once in college, the most important tournament of my undergrad career. It was for the national championship. She kicked my then overly cocky behind." He ignored Bryce's raised brow that pointedly took issue with how far in the past Niko's arrogance was. "I guess I can't say I know her exactly. We never talked outside of that one very significant college encounter. So needless to say, I am going to need a résumé on her ASAP, got it?" He continued reading for a bit, then looked up to make sure he had Bryce's attention. "Beginning with the answer to the question of how she moved here, gathered signatures and secured the Democratic Party nomination without me or someone in my family knowing about it."

"I gave you the names of those seeking both the Democratic and Republican noms months ago."

"Her name totally slipped by me. Didn't recognize it at all. Guess I was too focused on building my independent platform."

"Well, buddy, you know it now." Bryce nodded toward the paper. "How she did it, and why her candidacy is potentially problematic, is all there in black and white." He replied to a text message and stood. "I have a meeting with a couple pastors about your speaking to their congregations. Let's talk after you finish the article and discuss how you want to handle this unexpected development."

"All right. Will do."

Niko's gaze was speculative as he turned toward the window that looked out onto one of Paradise Cove's busiest streets. In the heart of downtown, he'd opted to run his campaign from this virtual epicenter where 75 percent of the businesses were located instead of from the stately offices of Drake Realty Plus, located closer to the Golden Gates community. So far the move had proved highly beneficial. On any given day he rubbed shoulders with company owners and their staff, and customers of the gift stores; art gallery and framing shop; travel agency; insurance companies; coffee shop; medical and dental offices; dog-grooming service; floral shop; New York–style deli; and middle-to-upscale boutiques. Once or twice a week he made sure to eat at Acquired Taste, one of the larger restaurants in the city, and made an equal amount of appearances at The Cove Café, the town's casual diner.

With six months to go until the election, he felt he'd locked up at least 60 percent of the vote. The other opponents weren't exactly lightweights, but didn't carry Niko's kind of clout. Monique was new in town. No one knew her. "Who in the heck is Mo Slater?" he'd asked himself when reading the name. Some local nobody, he vaguely remembered thinking. With almost no name recognition, how did she figure she could compete against one of the town's most popular native sons? The Republican candidate, Dick Schneider, had the seniors, Buddy Gao, a Libertarian, the fringe element. Which only left everybody else: the liberal Democrats, progressives, independents, those fifty-nine and younger and most of the town's female population. One would be shortsighted to leave out this pivotal bloc of voters.

As far as he'd been concerned a mere ten minutes ago, this election was in the bag. That was until Monique Slater, the only woman who'd beaten him at almost anything, had entered the picture and put a hitch in the proverbial giddy-up. He'd dismissed that guy named Mo with a wave of his long, thick well-groomed fingers. But not this woman;

not Monique. He'd underestimated her once before and paid the price.

Never again.

Picking up the paper once more, he studied the image smiling back at him. She was prettier than he remembered; softer, more feminine. Perhaps it was because in this photo her shoulder-length hair fell in soft curls around her face and neck, and her smile was bright and welcoming. The day of the debate, which was coming back to him as if it were yesterday and not over a decade ago, she'd worn her hair in a bun secured at the nape of her neck, as stark and conservative as the dark-colored pantsuit she'd also worn. Niko's thoughts whirled as he continued to study her picture. The more he thought about it, the more he realized that aside from the debate question and the fact that she blew his argument to smithereens, he didn't remember much else about her. Had they even had a conversation beyond the stage? He didn't think so. He remembered being angry and embarrassed at being out-argued, especially for the national trophy. The team had tried to ease his guilt and humiliation through teasing. A steely glare and a curtly delivered message left no doubt that for him there was no humor in any part of the affair. That night, he'd returned to California and walked straight into the arms of his latest love interest, one who'd undoubtedly been all too ready to offer comforting hugs and warm kisses to make him feel better. In time, this solid trouncing became a distant memory in what was otherwise a stellar debating record and career during a fun-filled, sexually adventurous four undergrad college years.

His thoughts returned to Monique. She was attractive, but off-limits. Aside from the obvious improprieties of dating a political opponent, she seemed hardly his type. Serious. Conservative. That was what he remembered.

Probably more than ready to give him a run for his considerable money. He hoped things wouldn't get ugly but would be prepared for all outcomes. Because winning the mayoral seat was only the first rung in the ladder of success he'd envisioned since attending the inauguration of the country's first African-American president. So whether or not he would win and begin this political climb was not something up for debate.

Monique took one final look in the mirror before stepping from the master bath in her newly purchased two-bedroom condominium and entered the spacious adjoining suite. She'd been very pleased to snag one of the few remaining units in the stylish Seventh Heaven complex, located adjacent to the more upscale community of Golden Gates and a mere three blocks from the neighborhood's award-winning golf course. That she'd been able to purchase anonymously had been even more satisfying and part of the larger plan to catch her mayoral competition totally by surprise. It was also why, until this week, no pictures of herself had accompanied the ads, articles and scant required information on Mo Slater. If what she'd been able to gather from her godmother was any indication, she'd totally succeeded.

A small smile danced across her face as she entered her walk-in closet and reached for the garment hanging on a wall hook. It was one of her power suits, simply designed and tailored to perfectly fit her five-foot-seven, toned-yet-curvy frame. She ran a hand over the soft fabric, a light wool blend in charcoal-gray, and imagined the look on Niko Drake's face when he saw the morning paper. Her assistant had rushed out before 5:00 a.m. to get a copy of the *Cove Chronicle* and had brought it over before Monique had enjoyed her first cup of joe, which she had, immensely. The well-written article officially announced her winning the Democratic vote for mayor and explained in clear, concise detail why she was the best person for the job of running the affairs of Paradise Cove.

Donning the Victoria's Secret lingerie that made her feel sexy and girlie beneath the ultraconservative pantsuit, Monique thought back to that first conversation she'd had almost two years ago with Margo Gentry, her godmother and the one who'd approached her with the idea of running for mayor on the Democratic ticket. Her first reaction had been a resounding no, followed by several reasons why the idea was impossible: too many cases, too many clients, no desire to enter politics and no desire to move from metropolitan Los Angeles. Margo had listened and then, in her gentle way, had reminded Monique of her godfather's expressed wish before he passed. This reminder had caused Monique to give the request due consideration. She dearly loved her father, but the sun had risen and set on her godfather, Claude. Mr. Slater was a reserved, serious, hardworking man who rarely laughed or showed affection. Growing up, he was the provider and authority figure who demonstrated love in practical ways. Claude Gentry was colorful, boisterous, sympathetic and infinitely supportive of the career he'd encouraged Monique to pursue. As a retired attorney, he could relate to her educational and career challenges and had offered sage advice that helped her successfully navigate the legal field. The one goal he'd dreamed of but never achieved was becoming mayor of the city he'd helped found, the goal that before dying he'd asked Monique to complete.

Not long after this poignant moment, a series of events made moving away and taking a break from law an attractive idea. She posted her candidacy just days shy of the cutoff for nominees, hired her godfather's best friend's grandson as her campaign manager and then silently and strategically began building her base, her funders and the focus of her campaign.

The results had come in just one week ago. Due to their hard work and her godmother's considerably liberal social circle, she'd secured the highest number of signatures and therefore the Democratic nomination for the mayoral race. Her very first thought after this confirmation? That she and Niko Drake would be squaring off once again. With even higher stakes this time.

A ringing cell phone brought her out of her musings. Monique looked at the caller ID and forced a smile into her voice. The woman on the other end of the line was known as a busybody who seemed to know, or think she knew, a little something about everybody in town. But she also owned the most popular salon, one that boasted nail care, facials, lash extensions and massages along with hair treatment, and one that was visited by women of all classes and colors. Joy DeWitt's active participation in her campaign could help Monique swing the female vote to her favor, and when it came to taking away women voters from Niko Drake's side, Monique knew that she'd need all the help she could get.

"Good morning, Joy," she answered, placing the call on speakerphone. "Are we all set for my visit?"

"My girls passed out flyers all last night, and with our offering twenty percent off all services except hair appointments, I expect the shop will be full all day."

"That sounds great. I really appreciate your help."

"You're welcome," Joy responded before lowering her voice and adding, "Helping you beat Niko Drake will be my pleasure."

The two chatted a few more moments and then Monique hung up the phone. She thought about the story that Joy had shared about why she detested the Drakes. She had given strong consideration as to whether or not she should have someone with such animosity as a visible supporter. At the end of the day, it came down to this fact: stopping short of something illegal, the ends justified the means.

After a last look in the walk-in closet's full-length mirror, Monique grabbed her oversize bag and set of keys and was out the door. She pointed the remote lock toward her newly leased luxury hybrid sedan and ignored the slight drizzle of rain as she headed toward the center of town. Ten minutes and she was there, having to park down the block for the amount of cars already lining the street, cars of customers who were no doubt in Joy's shop, enjoying the catered-in breakfast burritos, Danishes, juice and tea that had been provided and waiting to hear what Monique had to say.

"Let's do this, girl," she mumbled, encouraging herself as she locked her car, popped open her umbrella and began the short walk to the salon. "You've beaten Mr. Niko Drake once before. Let's see if you can do it again."

Chapter 2

Niko left the men laughing as he exited the chair from his weekly haircut at the barbershop. That he'd given up his personal in-home treatment in favor of this public establishment had proved a good political move. Roy wasn't as good with a pair of clippers and scissors as the barber who regularly came to the Drake estate and groomed all the men, but the camaraderie he'd established with Roy's regulars, along with the votes he'd likely garnered as a result, was worth a temporary trade-off from being pampered inside the Drake estate walls. After leaving a generous tip and a supply of promotional campaign cards, he walked to his sports car and, after another stop, made quick work of the few blocks that separated the barbershop and the beauty salon that he also visited weekly, a shop co-owned by an ex-girlfriend and her mother. Later, when the weather warmed, he'd do more walking, but on a cool and damp day like today, he was glad not to have to.

He neared Joy's House of Style and immediately noted more cars than usual. "Hmm, wonder what's going on here?" he pondered aloud, looking for a close parking space and finding none. *The word has probably gotten out that I show up most Saturdays,* he thought with a wry smirk. No better marketing than word of mouth. He looked in the backseat and wished he'd bought more than the two dozen roses he'd picked up on the way here, a practice he'd begun during his first visit, when a vendor selling flowers had come into the shop. He'd bought the lot and given them out to every woman present. So as not to be seen as chauvinistic or pandering toward these women, he'd coined a phrase. "Women are like flowers," he'd say as he shared them. "There's more to you than just the bloom."

Two steps into the shop and three things assailed him: the chatter of what sounded like dozens of women, the smell of food and a nearly life-size poster—okay, maybe he was exaggerating a bit but…wow—of his latest mayoral rival. Below the image of a smiling Monique Slater wearing a conservative black suit and a pleasant smile against a backdrop of law books and the American flag were the words *New Mayor, New Vision, New Day*. He'd barely had time to drink in the changes to the lobby when he heard applause coming from the back of the shop.

"Good morning, Niko!"

So caught up was he in all of these changes, he'd not even noticed the attractive receptionist always ready to flirt. He walked over to where she sat behind the receptionist counter. "Hello! Looks like you guys started the party without me."

"You're late, Mr. Mayor," the receptionist purred, batting stark blue eyes and flipping thick, raven-colored hair over her shoulder. "Someone beat you to us this morning, and if the impression she's making on our customers is any indication…you just might have a fight on your hands."

"Oh, really?" Niko leaned forward, his eyes twinkling as he asked in a conspiratorial tone, "Who's dared to come into my territory and challenge me?"

"I have."

The unexpected declaration from behind him threw Niko for an unexpected loop. But only temporarily. Within seconds he'd regrouped, turning around and greeting his opponent with a sincere smile.

"Monique Slater," he said, walking toward her with hand outstretched. "It's good to see you again."

Monique's brow rose. "Is it?" She returned his handshake, firm and assured. Her eyes held a saucy mixture of intelligence and tease. "I wasn't sure you'd remember our one and only former meeting." She continued, her voice lowered so that only Niko could hear. "As I remember, things didn't fare too well for you that day. Come November, I'm planning a similar outcome."

"I'm sure you are," Niko smoothly replied, allowing just a hint of bass into his voice. "I, on the other hand, am confident that there will be a very different ending. Though I must admit, your surprise strategy was quite effective, at least with me." To her arched eyebrow he further explained, "*Mo* Slater."

"Ah, yes. I was christened that in law school by a group of lovable jerks determined to make me hard as nails. They said Monique was too sexy, too feminine."

"You are that," Niko easily drawled.

Ignoring his comment, she replied, "Mo is friendly, casual, comfortable, a bit no-nonsense."

"And unisex."

"Yes."

A very attractive woman wearing jeans, a silk sweater and five-inch heels rounded the corner. "Oh, there you are!" she said to Monique with a grin.

"Hello, Joy."

"And with company, I see." For Niko there was no smile; hadn't been one since he'd broken up with her daughter, even though he and ex-girlfriend Ashley were on friendly terms. Joy turned back to Monique. "Some of the ladies who've offered to volunteer on your campaign wanted to know if you needed help today."

"That's very kind of them, but no, not today. Once they call the office, their names and contact information will be entered into our database, and they'll be assigned to the appropriate committee or team. I'll go back and explain myself so that they're clear."

Niko turned to the woman conspicuously ignoring him. "Hello, Joy. Didn't know you were helping the competition." He smiled. "But I'll still give you a rose."

He held one out to her. She refused it.

"Flowers are fine. But breakfast was better." She turned to Monique. "Mo, where did you get those breakfast burritos? And that sauce that tastes like grape jelly? Amazing!"

"From a caterer who came highly recommended," Monique responded. "I'm glad everyone enjoyed them."

"If you ladies will excuse me," Niko interrupted, not surprised at Joy's rudeness but a tad chagrined. Out publicly for mere hours and the new candidate was already trying to steal some of his shine. "I'll be on my way. Monique." He held out his hand. "I look forward to a fair, friendly, yet hard-fought race."

"You can count on it," Monique replied as Joy chuckled.

Niko nodded at both women, then turned the corner into the shop's main room. Soon, thoughts of what had just occurred were forgotten as he engaged the roomful of women in conversation. His topics shifted along with his personality; he was slightly flirtatious yet professional, down-to-earth yet knowledgeable, highbrow yet practical. Yes, this was a beauty shop, but some of the questions coming at him were intellectual and well thought out while others were simple and straightforward.

"We need more affordable housing," one woman boasting big plastic rollers said. "Everyone isn't wealthy like you. Do you have a plan for dealing with us regular folk?"

"What is your name, ma'am?"

"Diane," she stated with a smile.

"First of all, that is a very good question," he began after addressing her personally and embracing rather than running from the issue of his wealth. "The fact that my family has been very successful in the area of local real estate puts me in the very unique position of being able to personally help oversee this task. As many of you know, Drake Realty has been around almost as long as this town has been incorporated. We've worked hard to present a variety of living options based on consumer needs. As our town has grown and expanded, so has the diversity of its citizens. One of our latest projects was designed with this changing demographic in mind. The Seventh Heaven complex offers competitively priced housing, including condominiums, for our middle-income citizens. Now we're turning our focus to apartment buildings, for those in the low-to-mid-income range. I can't guarantee how large a supply we'll have at this level, but I do know that there will be some opportunity for renters, and those who'd like to buy a lower-priced home will have more variety from which to choose."

"Monique." The woman behind Diane looked over Niko's shoulder. He wasn't aware she'd come back into the main salon room. "Where do you live?"

"I purchased one of those middle-income condominiums that Niko spoke of," Monique answered. "In Seventh Heaven. Yet I'm also all too familiar with the myriad of families and working people who can't afford the homes in my neighborhood, and others for whom a community such as Golden Gates may as well be in Beverly Hills for the likelihood of their living there. In my practice as a defense attorney, I know what poverty and lack of opportunity can do for a neighborhood and to a soul. Paradise Cove is a beautiful part of California's landscape, and I'm here to ensure that every citizen, from the richest to the poorest, gets the chance to enjoy what you can currently afford, and to provide the resources so you can aim even higher."

"Ms. Slater is absolutely correct," Niko countered, using a debate tactic whereby the debater agreed with their opponent only to later use their very words to dismantle them. "The average person can't afford to live in the gated community my family helped develop. Starting with my grandfather, Walter Drake, we worked our butts off to establish and grow our company and used blood, sweat and tears to establish our brand. I have not nor will I ever either misrepresent who I am and where I come from, nor apologize for the blessings that this hard work has produced. The story of my family, who rose from humble Louisiana country beginnings to the top of the real-estate and architectural industries is one that is well-known to almost everyone with deep roots in Paradise Cove, and one that everyone who is new to our community will undoubtedly hear." He shot a friendly glance over at Monique and relaxed his stance. "I'm sure that Monique and I don't want to get into a debate about which of us cares more for all of the citizens of this community. It is clear that we both do. What you'll have to decide is who's best equipped to take us to a better future—someone born and raised in the midst of you or someone who's just arrived." He looked at his watch. "You ladies are as wonderful and intelligent as you are beautiful, and I'd love to spend more time answering your questions, but duty calls for me to move on to the next appointment. And considering that you were just given breakfast this morning, compliments of my opponent, I can't see why my office can't continue the gratuitousness set with these actions by offering everyone in the salon a fifty percent discount on their next salon visit. Just make the appointment with Joy and one of my staff members will be by next week to work out the details for receiving our matching payment."

The unofficial debate ended with women surrounding both Niko and Monique. He shook hands, signed marketing cards and gave hugs as he surreptitiously made his way to the front door, determined not to be late to the fundraising luncheon that had been organized by his staunchest supporter, his mother, Jennifer Drake. This event was as good an excuse as any for the whole family to get together. Quite frankly, Niko was looking forward to basking in their unwavering love.

"Thank you so much," he said to one ardent supporter, determined not to let her pass until she'd given him an enthusiastic hug.

"Send your concerns to my office," he heard from a little ways behind him. Monique was having just as hard a time leaving the packed salon as he was.

Finally they made it out of the crowd and onto the sidewalk.

"I guess that was our official beginning as political rivals," he said, calmly straightening the tan suit coat that he wore over a black button-down shirt and black jeans.

"I'm surprised you chose to enter into a debate," Monique responded, falling in beside him in a comfortable stroll toward their cars.

Niko's laugh was as hearty as it was genuine. "It's obvious that lone college victory gave you the confidence needed to throw your hat in the ring against me." He stopped, turned toward her. "But please understand. I'm no longer that inexperienced sophomore trying to make a name for himself in the academic community. I am now a confident, successful businessman with nothing to prove, who knows that hands down I am the perfect choice for mayor of Paradise Cove."

"Well," Monique said, reaching her car and pointing the remote to unlock it, "someone who's confident, successful and perfect surely has nothing to worry about." She got into her car, started the engine and rolled down the window. "Except for someone who's not at all intimidated by him. See you on the circuit, Niko," she finished, with a casual wave of her hand.

"Not so fast." Lightly grabbing the hand she'd just waved, he reached into the inside pocket of his jacket and produced a business card. "Let's keep in touch."

"Okay." She pulled her hand from his and took the card.

"Don't I get one?"

Monique eyed him for a second before reaching into her card case and handing him one.

"Thank you."

"You're welcome." She maneuvered her car out of the parking space and was gone.

Niko watched her car travel down the street, noting the Slater: Slated for Success and New Mayor, New Vision, New Day stickers that decorated her bumper. He walked the few yards to his own vehicle and got inside, trying to shake the feeling that he'd just been one-upped by Monique Slater. More than fifteen minutes later, as he pulled up to the entrance to Paradise Cove's exclusive Golden Gates community, he was still rattled. If he didn't know any better, he'd swear that the ultraconfident, business-savvy sister had just thrown down the gauntlet. Niko exited his car and walked toward his parents' front door, feeling more than ready, willing and able to accept Monique's challenge. The next time he saw her, he had only two more words to say before pulling out all the stops: *game on*.

Chapter 3

She thought she'd prepared herself, had felt she was ready for being face-to-face and up close and personal with the devilishly handsome Niko Drake. But the truth of the matter was that seeing him in person after so many years had almost taken her breath away, had brought back all of those girlie feelings of the secret college crush she'd had from the moment she'd first laid eyes on him in the auditorium on the day of their debate. A crush that she'd hidden, not only because of her introverted nature and inexperience but also because Niko had barely given her the time of day. Outside of their arguments, he hadn't shared a word with her and after an obligatory handshake had left the stage without a backward glance.

She'd gone back to her room, fired up her computer and learned everything about him that was online: about his successful family and deep roots in Northern California and about his love of sports and being a member of the college tennis team. In the ten years since their last meeting, she'd conducted an online search from time to time and checked out the images available. There were lots of them, mostly society related, with him attending this star-studded fundraiser or that charity ball, almost always with a stunning model type by his side.

It was in these moments that she'd push the old crush

back to the recesses of her memory, where it belonged. She wasn't a match for him then, and even now, with workouts, fashion consultants and career success, she still didn't feel that she was his type. Although the other points were legitimate, having to regularly see and interact with Niko was the single main reason why when Margo first approached her about living in Paradise Cove, let alone running for mayor, she'd balked. It had been enough to keep him off her mind while hundreds of miles apart. But now? Having to not only see him but interact, hobnob and, at times, debate? Really, she'd done some crazy things in her life: ziplined, parasailed, bungee jumped; she'd even participated in a flash-dance mob in New York's Times Square. But purposely create a life that had her in constant proximity to her college crush? One who'd gotten even finer in the past ten years? One who by just grabbing her hand had almost brought her to orgasm? What the heck was she thinking?

There was only one other person on the planet who'd known how Monique felt about Niko during those years, Monique's college roommate, Emma White. They'd gotten along famously during those years. After graduation, Mo continued on to law school while Emma married her college sweetheart. Distance and lifestyle kept them from regular meetings, but they maintained a close friendship through phone calls and emails. Emma was quiet, smart and filled with a good dose of small-town Midwestern common sense that made her wise beyond her years. Monique felt she could use that type of wisdom right now.

She looked at her watch. *Thirty minutes before my meeting with the farmers association.* She pulled into a parking lot and dialed up Emma. Hearing her good friend shout at children in the background made her instantly feel better.

"Sorry about that, Monique. The holy terrors are placing their emphasis on the last word today."

"Ha! In the throes of some imagined story line, no doubt."

"You know them too well."

"Who are they playing today?"

"Thor and Odin, this week's superheroes. I'm trying to convince them to move their battlefield from my living room to the backyard before something gets broken!"

"Sounds like a plan, and they sound like a handful. How are you, Em?"

"Currently, I'm under the belief that I've lost all semblance of sanity and control."

"Why?" Monique asked, with concern.

"Because as crazy as these boys have made us, we've decided to do it again."

"Do what again?"

"Uh, that wasn't a trick question, Ms. Attorney. Surely you can follow that clue."

"You're pregnant!"

"Bingo! Now there's the brain that helped my friend pass the bar first try."

"Okay, I'll admit I'm sometimes slow when it involves family business. Plus, you and Steve swore that you were… How did you guys put it?"

"Two and through."

"Exactly."

"And we meant it. But looks like a little sperm wiggled its way past my totally tied tube, joined forces with an errant egg and now Hunter and Cody are about to have a sibling."

"Boy or girl?"

"Don't know yet, but we're hoping for the latter."

"I'm happy for you, Em."

"Thanks, Monique. But enough about me. What's going on with you?"

"I guess you could say I've lost my mind, too. I took a leave from my job at the firm and am running for mayor."

"Oh, my gosh! You're running for mayor of Los Angeles?"

"Ha! My goals are lofty but not quite that high. It's a small town of almost four thousand people in Northern California, called Paradise Cove."

Silence. Crickets. For a full five seconds.

"Em?" Monique looked at her phone. "You still there?"

"I'm here. And this is the first time I've been speechless since Steve proposed to me at the top of a Six Flags roller coaster." Monique could hear Emma bustling around and imagined that she chewed her lower lip, something her friend was prone to do when thinking. "Okay, first question. Where in the heck did you get such a cockamamy idea to quit your job and run for mayor, and secondly, where is Paradise Cove?"

"Long story short, it was my godfather's dying wish. He ran for mayor twice and lost. During one of our last conversations before he passed, he asked if one day I'd give it a shot. To appease him I said yes, but didn't take the request that seriously. Margo, my godmother, did. When the man who's been mayor for the past twelve or more years decided not to run for reelection, she called and reminded me of my promise. Paradise Cove is a small yet impressive community in Northern California, a little more than an hour southeast of San Francisco."

"What's the name again?"

"Paradise Cove."

"Why does that name sound familiar?"

"Because over the years it's one I've probably mentioned a time or two as the place where Niko Drake was born and still resides."

"Right." The word came out slowly and dripped speculation. "Very interesting. Do tell me more."

"Well, I established residency about a year ago and moved into my condo here a few months later."

"A year ago? And you're just now telling me?"

"I thought I'd sent a text saying I'd moved."

"Yes, and that's all it said. I assumed it was across town, not out of town, and certainly not to your heartthrob's neck of the woods."

Monique sighed. "I didn't say anything more at first because I wasn't sure I'd get the nomination. Once that looked likely, my hands were full with relocating, closing out or reassigning cases and the election. And, by the way, he's not my heartthrob."

Emma chuckled. "No worries, Mo. I totally understand. So you're the Democratic candidate?"

"Yes, it's official as of this past week. I ran a very secretive campaign until I locked up the ticket."

"Why?"

"I wanted to secure the nomination before officially coming out, thereby enjoying the element of surprise."

"Did it work?"

"For months I've been able to quietly campaign under the radar. Now that the announcement has been officially released in the town's newspaper…we'll see."

"What about the man who you insist isn't your heartthrob? Have you seen him?"

"Yes."

"And?"

"I totally wanted to jump his bones, though I tried to appear unmoved."

The women cracked up.

"It's a very small town. I'll be seeing quite a bit of him from now until the election in November."

"Wait a minute. What does Rob think about all this? Did he move, too?"

"Well, that's the other thing. We broke up."

"No! From what you told me, he seemed like such a nice guy."

"He is a very nice guy and will make someone a wonderful partner. Just not me."

"What happened?"

"I loved him, Emma. But I wasn't in love. Once I made the decision to move to Paradise Cove, I also decided to end a relationship that really wasn't working."

A few seconds passed. Monique imagined Emma was digesting this news. "Monique, are you sure that the breakup with Rob wasn't because of your age-old crush on Niko?"

"Girl, I've already admitted he's hot, but any type of infatuation dissipated a long time ago."

"Hmm, if you say so."

"I say so."

"Your life is nothing if not interesting. Moves, breakups, running for office. Reconnecting with Niko sounds promising," Emma cooed, with a smile in her voice. "Rob's a nice guy, but Niko Drake is a really nice guy, and superhandsome to boot. You guys might even start dating."

"Debating, not dating."

"Why? Is he married?"

"Not as far as I know."

"Then who knows what the future holds?"

"Niko is my opponent, Emma. He's running for mayor, too."

"Oh, Lord."

"Earlier we held a debate. Our first in over ten years." She filled her in on the morning's impromptu meeting. "I must have been crazy to agree to this madness. May my godfather rest in peace."

"Let's not draw any hasty conclusions. This might be just the perfect setting to finally snag the man you've been in love with since college."

"Emma White, stop the foolishness! I am not nor have I ever been in love with Niko Drake."

"Is that why you've only dated a handful of guys since I've known you, and why you dragged poor Rob along for the past, what, three or four years?"

It was true. Monique and Rob Baldwin had met at a First Fridays event and bonded over lattes and shared political views. They'd begun dating not so much because Monique was head over heels but, well, because he was a good, decent man and because he was there. She no longer had to worry about who would escort her to office parties or industry events. She had someone with whom to share dinners, movies and occasional trips. He was safe and predictable, which up until Niko Drake had reentered her thoughts had suited her just fine. She'd never admit this truth, of course, not even to herself.

"Rob is a grown man. Had he been unhappy with our status, he could have left at any time."

"Sounds like you were the unhappy one. But—" Monique heard a loud crash. "Monique, I've got to go. The boys staged their joust indoors, and once again, as I feared, my china has been the only thing defeated."

"I don't know how you do it. Let me let you go be mommy."

"I will, but not before I give you what you called for even if it's not what you asked for."

"What's that?"

"Sound advice." Emma paused, and Monique found herself leaning toward the car's speaker so as not to miss a single word. She shouldn't have worried. There were only a few of them, delivered in that no-nonsense Midwestern style that Monique loved.

"Stop overthinking the situation. If you get a chance at what you really want, take it. And this campaign and your running for mayor is not what I'm talking about."

Chapter 4

Monique was still pondering her good friend's words when mere seconds later her phone rang again. "Monique Slater." She looked at her watch and, with only ten minutes before the farmers meeting, started her car and drove out of the lot where she'd stopped to call Emma.

"Hello, Monique. It's Niko."

The way her body reacted to the sound of his voice was totally unexpected. Muscles tightened in obscure places and butterflies lined her stomach walls. *Breathe, Monique.* She did, and a good thing, too. Hard to drive a car if one passed out.

"Niko. I guess it shouldn't have been unexpected, but I am surprised to hear from you."

"You're right. After asking for your card, hearing from me should have been totally expected."

There it was again, those squiggles traveling from her core to her vagina and bursting within. His voice, deep and soothing, swept over her like a Southern summer breeze, causing inappropriate mental pictures to float through her mind. And try as she might to turn away these thoughts and focus on practicality and politics and Paradise Cove, all she could imagine right now was the strong, tall body she'd admired earlier that day hovering naked over hers.

Shaking her head to rid herself of the images, she spoke

with a forced casualness and calm. "What can I do for you, Mr. Drake?"

The length of his pause made her immediately regret—or was it applaud?—the way she'd worded the question.

"There are several possibilities that come to mind," he finally responded, his voice one of professionalism while Monique imagined that his thoughts were anything but. "However, joining me for dinner is my first request."

"Thank you for the offer, Niko, but I'm not sure our being seen dining together is such a great idea. We are adversaries, after all."

"We don't have to be. There's nothing wrong with two people going after the same goal doing so while getting along. It's one of the reasons I'd like to talk with you. This morning our meeting was unexpected. We jumped into a debate almost before we said hello. I didn't have the opportunity to congratulate you on your stellar law career or even welcome you to Paradise Cove."

Monique reached her destination, a plain, small building in Paradise Valley, a farm community of rolling hills, herds of cattle and, most recently, vineyards, just east of the incorporated town of Paradise Cove. She pulled into a gravel-coated parking lot already filled mostly with Dodge and Ford pickups and SUVs.

She turned off her motor, checked her phone and saw that the meeting began in five minutes. "I'm heading into a meeting but have a minute or two." Silence. "Niko?"

She was rewarded with his laughter, rich and throaty and filled with genuine cheer. In spite of herself she could imagine his smile, could see his sparkling teeth and the hint of a dimple in his left cheek. Today she'd noticed how perfect his lips were, and right now thoughts of what else those lips could do besides form a coherent sentence were about to be her undoing.

"I like your style. Quick and to the point, straight, no chaser. But I'm more deliberate in my approach and would really appreciate the opportunity to congratulate you in person. Say tonight, around seven or eight o'clock?"

"Fine," Monique said, having once again glanced at her watch as two more cars drove up and the occupants went inside. "Text me where you'd like to meet. Eight o'clock is fine."

"Thanks, Monique. I look forward to seeing you tonight."

She tried to hide it, tried to put on her professional, *I'm-totally-in-control* face as she entered the open room and began to shake hands. But her insides were smiling as if she'd just won a case. She continued to fool herself and act as though tonight's dinner was just another necessity on the political trail.

But deep down, Monique knew better. And if she didn't... her heart did.

Niko walked to the door of his father's study, where he'd gone to make the call to Monique in private. Now that he'd done what had been on his mind since arriving at his parents' fundraiser, coordinated the plans to see her again as soon as possible, he felt that maybe he could totally focus on the dozens of well-wishers milling around to ensure a November win.

One of Niko's younger brothers, Terrell, who was also one of the family's busybodies, saw him as he stepped out of the office and closed the door. "Is it all set?"

Niko placed his arm around Terrell's shoulders as they walked toward the great room and adjoining pool and patio area, where most of the crowd had gathered. "Is what all set, brother?"

"That hot date for tonight."

"What date?" Niko removed his arm and gave his brother an innocent look.

"The one that had that cheesy grin on your face when you closed the door. I saw it. And I know that look, man. It was the 'I got this' grin," Terrell continued, using air quotes. "The victory smile when you're going in for the score."

"Are we talking about women or sports? Show respect, son," Niko replied with a slap on the back, thankful to see his parents as soon as he turned the corner. Terrell's sure-to-be-sarcastic response would have to wait for another time.

Niko's parents, Ike Sr. and Jennifer, were talking to their neighbors who owned several manufacturing plants around the country. Their citizen advocacy organization was one of the largest contributors to Niko's campaign.

"We were just talking about you," Jennifer said, beaming as her son approached.

"All good, I hope." Niko shook hands with the husband and hugged the wife.

"Well, son, that depends on how you feel about locking up the vote from the manufacturers union."

Niko again shook the neighbor's hand, exclaiming, "That's good news indeed!"

For the next two hours, he and his family made the rounds, quietly encouraging huge bids for items being sold during the silent auction. His parents went well beyond their goal of raising a million dollars for their son's campaign. After a short speech and a quick toast thanking the guests for their presence and support, Niko begged off the continued requests for his charismatic presence, citing another engagement. That the engagement was with the very woman this group's funding would help him beat was—for him—beside the point. Ever since their phone call and her agreeing to dinner, the serious yet sexy Monique Slater hadn't been far from his mind.

"Nicodemus!"

Niko had reached the marble-floored foyer but stopped at the sound of his mother's voice. Aside from his grandparents and very occasionally his father, his mother was the only one who called him by his given name. And usually only when she had something very serious, or chiding, to convey. He took a breath to prepare himself and turned around.

"Yes, Mother?"

"I just wanted to remind you about tomorrow's Sunday brunch. It's been almost a year since I've had almost all of my children in one zip code, and I want everyone at the table."

"You've already reminded me, Mom, remember? Don't worry. I'll be there."

"Well," she said, straightening the silk tie that perfectly matched his tailored suit, "I'm just making sure."

"What would make you think I'd not come after giving my word?"

Jennifer's voice dropped. "Whatever or whoever has you almost running from a very successful fundraiser with a gleam in your eye."

Geez, am I that obvious? Maybe, but once again Niko answered by not answering. He kissed his mother on the forehead. "Thank you so much for everything you did today. Without your great taste and keen eye, this affair would not have been nearly as successful."

Jennifer chuckled. "Nice try, son, but I don't distract so easily. Feel free to have her join us if you'd like."

"Goodbye, Mother. See you tomorrow."

"Love you, son."

"I love you more."

Walking to the car, his phone rang. "Hello, Ashley."

"Hey. What are you doing?"

"Just left a fundraiser, now headed home to change before going to dinner."

"Then my timing is perfect. I haven't eaten, either. Tell me where you're going and I'll meet you there."

"This is a business dinner."

"Oh, okay. Listen, I wanted to thank you for the generous arrangement you made with our customers earlier today. We're booked solid for the next two weeks."

"My newest mayoral rival provided breakfast. I had to step up my game."

"Mo Slater? She's been cozying up to my mom, who's taken the bait. I think she's an opportunist, and I think you have nothing to worry about."

"I appreciate that."

"So…what are you doing after dinner?"

"I have plans but appreciate your support. Take care, Ashley."

Niko loosened his tie as he arrived at his home, mere blocks away from his parents' abode. He thought about what his grandfather had told him when he'd shared his plans to enter politics.

"Your life won't be your own," Walter Drake had told him, a few terms as city councilman in his native New Orleans giving him a personal perspective from which to speak. "Your time, either. Get ready for everyone to want a piece of you. But being a dedicated public servant has its own unique rewards."

Niko had listened keenly to his grandfather, who he now counted as one of his most valued political consultants. On one thing Niko most definitely agreed. There were rewards to throwing one's hat into the political ring. Niko wondered if there was any possibility that tonight's date could prove to be one of them.

Chapter 5

Monique stepped inside the entrance to the exclusive Paradise Cove Supper Club, located just inside the city's equally elite golf course available by membership only. While not an avid golfer, she'd been to the course and had also dined at this restaurant. Thanks to her godmother, she knew firsthand about the skillful hands of its classically trained Brazilian chef, who loved to add new twists to traditional dishes. She also made sure she dressed to impress, and this time she didn't even lie to herself about the reason. Niko was why she'd chosen the never-before-worn Calvin Klein sheath dress that was simple but tailored to fit like a glove, caressing but not squeezing every one of her curves. The royal-blue color highlighted her deeply tanned skin, and the softly rounded neckline, jeweled choker and gently upswept hair with wisps remaining against the crook of her neck gave special emphasis to that area. She'd kept her makeup minimal—a dusting of powder, mascara and gloss—letting her designer silver slingbacks adorned lightly with crystals provide just the right amount of understated bling.

"Good evening." The genteel-looking man made a slight bow as he greeted her.

He was so formal in his demeanor that Monique almost

felt she should curtsy in response. Instead, she graced him with a smile. "Good evening."

"Forgive my presumptiveness, but a woman as beautiful as you is surely not dining alone. Are you perhaps here to meet Mr. Drake?"

"I am," Monique responded, hiding her surprise. "Has he arrived?"

"He has indeed, Ms. Slater, and instructed me to have you join him at once. Please, come this way."

Monique held her smile, discreetly looking around the restaurant and nodding at those who met her eye. She was also trying to see Niko, trying to get in that first look, the one that seemed to take her breath away no matter how often she saw him. But they walked through the entire main restaurant and she hadn't seen a trace. When the maître d' turned down a short hallway, Monique was even more confused. *I wasn't aware of another section. This place must be bigger than I thought.*

They reached an ornately decorated set of brass double doors. The maître d' knocked twice, paused a couple of seconds and then turned the knob. "After you," he said, holding the door as he stood back.

Monique walked through the door and was immediately grateful for the discipline that allowed her to calmly watch as Niko stood next to a table set for two and continue the steps to meet him. Especially when her insides quivered, her panties instantly moistened and once again the air managed to leave the room. He was handsome. Even a blind woman could see that. But living in L.A. and spending as much time on the beach as her schedule allowed, she saw gorgeous, well-chiseled Adonises all the time. What was it about this man, Monique wondered, that made her lose all semblance of control? It was a trait that had served her well all of her life and now it was as if she couldn't even spell the word let alone possess an ounce of its attributes. The room was small and intimate, yet in the steps it had taken to reach him she'd been able to steady her breathing and find her tongue.

"Good evening," she said, holding out her hand. "Thanks again for inviting me to dinner."

After giving an almost imperceptible nod to the maître d', Niko enveloped her small, dainty hand in his strong, masculine one before lifting it to his lips for the wispiest of kisses. "The pleasure is all mine, Ms. Slater." He stepped away from her and pulled out her chair. "Please."

She sat, trying very hard not to imagine that she was Cinderella and Niko her prince. "Thank you."

She lowered her head to place the napkin on her lap. But that didn't stop her from stealing a couple of discreet glances as he walked over to his chair and sat down. She noticed that he too had changed from the flattering slacks, shirt and pullover that he'd worn at the beauty salon. The navy-colored suit that now graced his body was immaculate and looked so soft that she wanted to squeeze his arm. Not only to touch the fabric but to see if the biceps she'd perceived beneath the cloth was real. In a field dominated by men wearing nice suits, she should have not been bothered in the slightest. But there was something about Niko that made him stand out. It was the combination, she decided, smiling over her glass as she took a sip of water. Looks, brains, money and class mixed with just the right amount of swagger and sex appeal. Lethal. Dangerous. And damned if she didn't want to go ahead and play with fire, even knowing that there was a strong possibility that she could get burned.

"This is nice," she said into the silence, as she looked around to keep from connecting with the dark bedroom eyes that gazed upon her. "I didn't know this room existed."

"Not many do, unless you're a lifetime member. My parents have belonged to the club forever, so the children gained entry pretty much by default."

"How many children are in your family?" Monique eased back against the cushioned chair, thankful that she finally felt that she was in familiar territory—subtle interrogation.

"There are eight of us." Niko leaned back, as well. "All of us live here in Paradise Cove except for Reginald, whose wife has deep and abiding ties with New Orleans, where they reside, and my youngest brother, Julian, who's studying in New York." He took a sip of lemon water. "What about you?"

"One brother, a doctor. He practices at Johns Hopkins in Baltimore."

"A doctor and a lawyer, huh? Your parents must be proud."

"They are. Both were overachievers and encouraged their children to be the same. Are any of your siblings involved in politics?"

The smooth grin that spread across Niko's face was enough to make a nun rethink her celibacy. He looked absolutely decadent, Monique imagined, and she would have bet a year's salary he tasted just as sweet. "Come on, now. You're an attorney. We've both done our homework, scoped out the terrain. If there was another Drake involved in politics, that information would be on the internet, and you would know about it."

"Which is why I'm sure my brother's occupation is no surprise. Nothing wrong with including the question in a bit of friendly conversation, is there?" Monique's eyelashes fluttered as she looked at him, a move that was totally against the game plan. *Do not flirt with him, Monique Slater. Do. Not. Flirt!* Before this thought could completely make the rounds from her head to the body parts that needed the directive, a giggle had escaped her lips and she'd reached up to place an errant tendril of hair behind her ear.

Wait, was that me? Did I just giggle? I never giggle. I'm too old and too grown to giggle. She gave herself a silent chiding and vowed to behave.

Niko eyed her intently but said nothing as the sommelier entered the room and presented Niko's wine choice. After he tasted and nodded his approval, the handsome young blond nodded, turned on his heel and quietly left the room.

Pouring their glasses of wine hadn't taken long, but fortunately it had been enough for Monique to regain her professional-woman, top-notch defense-attorney senses. By the time he held up his glass, she was ready for those sexy brown eyes, cushy-full lips and dimple that winked every time that he smiled. Salivating, lust-filled, but ready.

She picked up her glass. "To what shall we toast?"

"What about to what was earlier suggested? A fair, clean, positive campaign?"

"Sure."

They clinked glasses and took small sips of the vintage-year cabernet.

Monique took a second drink and set down her glass. "You said that too fast for it to have been an off-the-cuff response."

"It's one of the reasons I invited you here. I know that modern-day politics have been reduced to negative ads and smear campaigns. But that's not my style. And while I don't know very much about you—the second reason why I requested the pleasure of your company—I get the feeling that it's not your style, either."

"I definitely plan to run on the merits of my education, experience and qualifications to lead this town into an exciting and prosperous future."

"What type of excitement do you have planned?"

There it was again, a flirtatiousness executed so deftly and gone so quickly that she questioned whether it was real or imagined. Perhaps this was just his personality and, as such, she shouldn't get her hopes up that he was interested in her in that way.

And just what way is that, Monique Slater? This question in her mind she heard in her mother's no-nonsense voice. It was a good question. Because Monique wasn't interested in Niko like that. She'd had a crush on him, sure. Probably along with thousands of other college-aged girls. She found him attractive. So what? Anyone with eyes would feel the same. But any thoughts of anything ever happening between the two of them were beyond wishful thinking; they were flat-out ridiculous. She wasn't his type, nor he hers if she really thought about it. Even though she'd ended their relationship, she belonged with a man more like Rob: solid, steady and...safe. And most of all? They were adversaries in a political campaign. It would be the height of scandal if anything untoward ever happened between them. No, their interactions would be totally innocent and strictly professional. How it should be. How it must be.

So why did this thought make Monique feel like crap?

"Strategizing against me?"

Monique looked up from the wineglass, where she'd been idly running her finger around the rim. She hadn't realized she'd grown silent, had no idea how long she'd been lost in her own thoughts. "Forgive me. There's a lot on my mind."

"Running for elected office is definitely hard work."

"I also have a couple cases to wrap up before I can immerse my head totally in the game."

"You're still handling clients?"

"I took a leave of absence from the firm but retained a couple cases that I felt too involved in to turn over. I'm also mentoring a young man who was paroled to my care. His name is Devante."

"He lives with you?"

Monique shook her head. "He and another young man share an apartment."

"That's dedication."

"Or narcissism. Right now, I can't tell which."

"Ha!" A waiter entered the room pushing a tray containing a bowl of wilted arugula salad and warm, freshly baked rolls. "I hope you don't mind that I took the liberty of planning our menu. The choices in here are different than those offered in main dining."

"Really? I'd looked forward to the chef's succulent filet mignon."

"Ah, so you're familiar with Esteban's culinary skills."

"Probably not as intimately as you are, but I really enjoy the way he prepares that cut of meat. I'm not that picky of an eater, however. I'm sure that whatever you've ordered is fine."

She enjoyed a bite of the salad that had been placed down in front of her. "This is delicious. I love the blend of sweet and bitter."

"Yes, that's one of Esteban's signature dressings, a pomegranate vinaigrette."

"So you're not only successful, but cultured, too."

"I guess you can say that my mama raised me right." Monique laughed and he continued. "We were always learning, school or no. The world was our classroom and it was always in session. She encouraged us to be curious, to ask questions and to not be afraid to try new things. Then, it wasn't always appreciated, but now I'm reminded of the foundation she and Dad provided every single day."

"Do you personally know the other men running? Dick Schneider and Buddy Gao?"

"Dick's a good old boy I've known for most of my life. He's old-school, traditional, conservative. His father's a retired judge with connections. Fortunately they're largely Republican while ours is a more liberal town."

"And Buddy?"

"Good kid, former immigrant reform activist who cut his political chops in Berkeley after graduating from the university there. He's only twenty-six years old, but will probably be a contender in the future."

"He's twenty-six and you call him a kid? How old are you?"

Niko smiled. "Thirty-one. My grandparents say I have an old soul. What about you? Or are you one of those women?"

"Thirty-three," she responded, ignoring his jab. "And, by the way, you do look good."

"Thank you," he responded, obviously appreciative of her remark.

"For an old man."

"Ha!"

The easy banter continued through an entrée of perfectly prepared chateaubriand served with grilled asparagus and jasmine rice, and a three-berry crisp with whipped cream for dessert. They talked generally about the political landscape and the upcoming national elections, but also learned a bit more about each other. Niko was pleased to learn that Monique was an avid tennis fan who played on occasion, and Monique found it interesting that the chic, fashion-forward Niko rode horses and liked to fish. One topic was pointedly not discussed: their romantic lives.

After being let out through a private side door, Niko walked with Monique through the parking lot. "Thanks again for a lovely evening," she said, after he'd insisted on opening her car door. She held out her hand.

He looked at it and then at her. "My roots are Southern," he said easily. "We prefer hugs to handshakes."

He took a step and in the next second she was enveloped in his strong, comfortable arms. As soon as her soft breasts met his hard chest, she felt it, an attraction so strong it was electric and real, traveling from her core to her toes and back up to her heart. Her nipples pebbled and once again muscles that hadn't been used for months tightened with desire, even as she felt her mouth go dry. Niko must have felt something too because he abruptly ended the hug and stepped back.

She didn't want to look at him, sure that blatant desire, ardent lust and thoughts of good old booty bumping showed on her face. But since it would seem even stranger to say goodbye with her face obscured, she did face him, totally prepared to see a cocky, knowing look in his eye.

But she saw something different—hunger, desire—before he blinked and the moment was gone.

"See you on the campaign trail," she sang, trying to sound casual and unaffected, getting into her car before she did something crazy like throw caution to the wind and kiss the lips that had tempted her all evening.

"Be safe," he responded.

She pulled away, then looked into the rearview mirror to find him still standing there, staring. Something had happened tonight, when they'd hugged; something innate yet palpable, something ethereal yet all too real. Monique had no doubt that she'd felt it and she was positive that Niko had sensed it, too.

On the drive home she tried to redirect her thoughts about him, focus solely on the fact that they were opponents in a coveted mayoral campaign. But such attempts were futile. The race was on, of that there was no doubt. Whether it ended in a boardroom or a bedroom, now, that was the question. That Monique was leaning toward the latter as her ending of choice was creating a problem, one that would only escalate in the coming months if there were more intimate meetings like this.

From now until November their seeing each other was a given. With that in mind Monique determined that it was best to keep her meetings with him as public and professional as possible. Because she could not be responsible for her actions with that man behind closed doors.

Chapter 6

The next day, Niko entered the Drake residence to the sound of raucous laughter floating down the hallway. He smiled, despite the fact that he had no idea who'd told the joke or caused the chuckles. It could have been anyone. When it came to Drake gatherings around the family table, they were always lively, filled with stimulating conversation and many differences of opinion. It was as though having a child to cover every possible angle of life's spectrum had been Ike Sr. and Jennifer's plan.

Take the oldest, Ike Jr. Almost from the womb, it was known that he'd be the one who'd step into his father's footsteps and carry on the family business. He'd taken to this role like a fish to water, had graduated with business degrees from Fisk University and the Wharton School and hadn't looked back. Reginald, the second son, was doing the same thing in their native home of New Orleans. As with Ike Jr., business had come naturally. So had family life. After spending time in California and giving relocation brief consideration, he'd married his college sweetheart and turned a nineteenth-century Creole town house into a modern-day masterpiece. Warren, the brother directly under Niko, took after his grandfather as a lover of the land. The first crop harvest from a vineyard he'd begun several years ago had turned a tidy profit and seemed poised to do it again. The twins, Terrell and Teresa, though currently working at the family business, were still figuring out exactly what they wanted to do in life. Armed with degrees in engineering and journalism respectively, and boasting fraternity and sorority connections and healthy bank accounts, the sky was the limit. Julian, next to the youngest, was the serious one in the bunch. As quiet and introspective as his siblings were the opposite, he'd not talked until he was two years old and even now spoke sparingly, usually when he had something to say that was prolific and profound. A personality that was perfect for psychology, his chosen profession. And then there was London, the baby of the family. She'd managed to stay out of trouble long enough to earn a degree in fashion design and she'd surely spent enough money on clothes to fund several college educations, but what she'd end up doing with her life was anyone's guess. He heard her now, arguing with their father about why he should buy her a house. Niko shook his head. His mother was right. The Drake bunch had been overdue for a get-together. He didn't realize how much he'd missed it until now.

"There he is!"

"About time you got here, boy."

"If it isn't the politician. Where you been? Out kissing babies and schmoozing old men?"

The questions came in rapid fire with one beginning before another could end.

"Will you all stop the interrogation?" Jennifer raised her voice above the din, quickly gaining the respect that she commanded. "Let the child sit down before you start in."

"Thanks, Mom." He kissed her and took a seat.

"Now," Jennifer said as soon as his butt had touched the cushion, "why are you so late getting to the brunch?"

"Geez!" Niko joined the others in laugher. He eyed the

drink pitchers on the table, deciding whether he wanted a Bloody Mary mix, lemonade or tea. Given how he was in the hot seat, he reached for the one containing alcohol. "I thought you were on my side."

"I am. I let you sit down, didn't I?"

"That, you did."

"Does your being late have anything to do with your date last night?"

Niko almost spewed the sip he'd just taken. Not even twelve hours later and his private dinner with Monique was already making the rounds?

Jennifer reached over and patted his hand. "Don't worry. This isn't fodder for the rumor mills. Grace hired Esteban for a dinner she's having tonight and happened by the club to share some last-minute changes she'd thought of for her menu. She saw you and Monique Slater leaving out the back door. Said you two shared a friendly hug."

Niko got up and walked to the buffet. "Did you talk to Grace or a reporter for the *Cove Chronicle?*"

Ike Sr. snorted. "Is there a difference?"

"Don't worry, Niko. I trust Grace to keep a confidence. She and I have been friends for decades."

"I appreciate that but there's no great story here. Yes, Monique and I met for dinner. For obvious reasons, we decided to do so privately."

"You don't owe us an explanation," Terrell said, rising from the table and joining his brother at the buffet. "She's an attractive, single woman. Oh, and she's breathing. Of course you'd take her out."

"That's low, bro," Warren said with a shake of his head. "And considering how many women's numbers are in your phone's address book, it's a dig that you should not be making. Don't listen to Terrell, baby," he said to his wife. "Drake men aren't players."

"Boy, please." London smirked while texting on her cell phone. "Considering how big Charli's stomach is getting, it looks like someone's had some fun."

"London!" Jennifer gave her youngest a look. "How many times do I have to tell you…no electronics at the table."

"Mom, it's just—"

"Put it down." Ike Jr. gave his younger sister a stare that dared her to defy him. She put down the phone.

Niko was glad the heat on him had been deflected and to know what Grace had seen. It was all the more reason why he couldn't see Monique socially or act out the fantasy that had played in his head ever since holding her in his arms. No, there were too many eyes, too many people watching. It wouldn't do for him to act on that desire at all.

Chapter 7

Monique blinked her eyes, allowing them to adjust to the bright sunlight. She was glad she'd taken her godmother up on her offer and attended church. It wasn't something she did often, but the choir had sung beautifully and she'd enjoyed the sermon. Sitting in those pews, listening to his lyrical cadence speak on the truth setting one free and unconditional love, she'd been assuaged with a feeling of peace. And then another feeling, guilt, about Rob and the message from him on her phone when she had returned home from dinner with Niko. How he missed her and wanted her to reconsider the decision to end their relationship. Finally considering his feelings was what had led her to break up with him in the first place.

As if conjuring him up, her phone rang. She pointed to it, mouthed "I'll be back" to Margo and stepped a few yards away from the socializing parishioners. "I was just thinking about you," she said by way of greeting, adjusting her earbud to hear more clearly.

"I hope it was about what I suggested on the message I left," Rob replied, his voice crisp and professional-sounding in her ear. "And how you'd like to invite me up to see you."

She immediately thought of Niko, and how words that oozed from his inviting lips caused her toes to curl. Rob had never caused anything to curl, tighten or moisten simply by speaking. Ever. It was true, yet she immediately chided herself for making the comparison.

"How's life in Los Angeles?"

"Same old, same old. Lonely without you."

Say "I miss you, too," Monique! She wanted to, but she couldn't. The words were blocked by thoughts of the pastor's message about truth and being set free. "I had my first debate with an opponent yesterday," she said instead.

"Really? Who?"

"Niko Drake. He's running as an independent."

"That was fast. Didn't you just announce your candidacy days ago?"

"Yes."

"Who set this up so quickly?"

"Would you believe the owner of a beauty shop?"

"Come again?"

Monique laughed, then shared the short version of yesterday's events. "We both held ourselves in check, didn't let things get ugly. Then last night we met and agreed to leave the negative ads and mudslinging to others and run positive-oriented races that stick to the facts."

"You met last night?"

Monique heard the pout in his voice and immediately recognized her error. "Yes." And then, to make it more official-sounding, she added, "We had a brief meeting."

"Interesting. Where?"

"At the golf-course country club." That was sort of, kind of, correct. It was the best she could do. Monique simply couldn't bring herself to share that Niko had treated her to a five-star meal in an extravagant private dining room.

"Hobnobbing with the bougie crowd, I see."

"I'm interacting with all of the citizens of Paradise Cove," Monique responded. "No matter the height of their status or the size of their bank account." She hadn't meant to sound curt, but she had.

"Of course you are, Monique. I didn't mean to imply otherwise. Listen, I'd like to come up next weekend. Maybe we can spend a night in romantic San Francisco."

"I'm afraid I won't see San Francisco until the Silver Serenade Concert during Memorial Day weekend. Until then, my schedule is filled with appearances, meetings and juggling clients."

"What is the Silver Serenade Concert?"

"It's a charity event put on by members of Northern California society, including Paradise Cove, a black-tie affair."

"Sounds like one that requires an escort. I'm offering my services."

"Rob…"

"We were friends before we began dating, Monique. Can't we be friends now?"

She hesitated, thinking. Was it a good idea to reconnect with him in this way? Would it send the wrong signal? And then she considered his words. They were friends. She could use an escort. This might be a way to maintain a friendship with a really nice guy.

"I think you'd really enjoy the concert, Rob. I'll get another ticket."

"I can purchase my own ticket, Monique."

"Sure you could. If you could find one. With the concert sold out, they're hard to get. If it means that much, you can pay me back."

"Deal. Send me the details. But I'd still like to see you this weekend. It's a rare one where I won't be working. Plus, you can help me celebrate."

"What?"

A pause and then "My birthday."

"So sorry, Rob! Of course your birthday is this weekend. With everything going on here I'd totally forgotten."

"So…can I come up?"

"Sure, why not."

"Excellent! I can't wait to see you!"

Monique immediately regretted her decision. From the excitement in his voice, she knew that he hoped for a second chance. When he arrived she'd have to make it crystal clear that she would not be his birthday present and that a reconciliation was never going to happen.

Looking up, she saw her godmother waving her over. "Rob, I've got to run. I'm taking Margo and two of her best friends out to lunch. Call you later?"

Shortly after hanging up from Rob, Monique and company headed to Acquired Taste, which, next to the golf-course supper club, was the city's nicest restaurant. The women were chatty and Monique was glad for the diversion. Thoughts of how impossible her rekindling a relationship with Rob was reminded her of how equally unlikely it was she'd begin one with Niko. If she defeated him in the election, then any chance of romance would go out the window. She still remembered how angry he'd been when she'd won the debate. He'd wanted nothing more to do with her. Would someone as proud as Niko date the woman who snatched his political dream? She didn't think so. If she lost, the outcome would be the same. No Niko. He'd be the town's darling and even more a target for determined female constituents. She'd go back to Los Angeles, pick up where she'd left off in her career and find a man who was as comfortable and loyal as the one she'd let go, but gave her the kind of excitement that the one who could never be hers did with just a glance.

Afternoon passed into evening and Monique remained within the confines of Golden Gates, where her godmother resided in one of the smaller homes near the community's north side. She enjoyed Margo's company immensely, but more than that, Monique didn't want to leave and be alone with her thoughts. So after eating at Acquired Taste, she had driven each of the ladies to their homes and then taken her godmother on a drive through the country before they'd returned to Margo's home and watched shows on Investigation Discovery. That superpositive Margo, who wouldn't hurt a fly, found ID to be one of her favorite channels, with back-to-back stories about murder and mayhem, was for Monique a complete irony. Still they watched and chatted and drank homemade hot chocolate. But when Margo began to yawn, having missed her usual midday nap, Monique gave a hug, said goodbye and headed out the door.

Still, Monique was not ready to face her empty home. So instead of getting in her car, she went around to the trunk, donned the sneakers always kept there for emergencies and decided to find and walk the trail that Margo had mentioned, the one that bordered the Golden Gates community and the government-protected marshland just on the other side. According to her godmother, a variety of rare birds and insects called this area home, so for now it was off-limits to land developers. Monique wondered how the Drakes felt about that as she breathed in fresh air and swung her arms, enjoying the impromptu exercise.

She continued to think about them as she reached the trail and began walking through it, now thankful for the government's intervention. This natural habitat was beautiful. The trail was lined with trees and branches that created a canopy overhead. Flowers bloomed and there were so many different leaves and bushes that after a dozen or so Monique lost count. She meandered for ten minutes, not knowing where the trail ended and not really caring. Even though it felt otherwise, she was only minutes from civilization. Right now she felt safe and secure in this cocoon of natural beauty, with the sounds of the insects and frogs serving as background music to the myriad of thoughts that continued to bounce around her head: the race, Rob, Niko, the Drakes and then...

Monique stopped dead in her tracks. What was that noise? She looked around, noticing for the first time that the light was fading and that total darkness was probably less than half an hour away. Swaying branches now cast creepy shadows across the smooth trail; the sound of insect noises seemed to increase. She looked ahead of her and then turned back, deciding that where she'd come from was a better trek to take than one into the unknown.

But there it was again. That sound. She paused again, and her heart beat louder than any other sound she currently heard. Now watching all of those crime shows about stalking and strangling and murders in swamps didn't seem like such a great idea. It was getting dark. The area was swampy. And she had the frightening and disconcerting feeling that she was not alone.

The sound became clearer. Footsteps. Definitely footsteps, coming closer and gaining speed. A jogger, perhaps? Or a serial killer? Rational thought fled, and Monique decided to do the same. She turned away from the footsteps, broke into a full-on run...and ran smack-dab into a hard chest, a scruffy chin and strong, sure arms around her.

She screamed.

"Monique! It's me!"

Through her haze of fear she heard the voice, remembered the owner of its sound as well as the scent of the cologne that had embraced her twenty-four hours before. Niko? She looked up. It was him!

"Niko!"

"Yes," he said, amid laughter.

The rumbling in his chest caused by his chuckling caused Monique to feel annoyed yet comforted at the same time. She pushed away from him.

"What's so funny?"

He allowed her to retreat, but still held on to her arms, his face a study in amusement. "When you said you'd see me on the trail," he drawled, looking square into her face with those bedroom eyes, "I didn't know that this is what you had in mind."

Chapter 8

Monique placed a hand on her chest and worked to slow both her breathing and her rapidly beating heart. "You scared me," she panted, glancing behind her. "I thought I heard someone running from that direction. I thought that..."

She turned around. There they were again. Footsteps. She was sure of it this time. "There's someone else out there!"

Monique made a move to go around Niko and away from oncoming danger. He placed a firm grasp on her arm, immediately stopping her progress. "Whoa, hold on, babe. It's okay."

Monique wasn't so sure. She looked behind her and could now clearly detect someone who'd stopped running but was now definitely walking their way. He looked menacing, dressed in all black and wearing shades even though it was evening. Instinctively, she backed up against Niko. Only her fear made her impervious to the feel of him against her, to the smell of his cologne wrapping itself around her body and the feel of his five-o'clock shadow against her temple.

"I don't like the looks of this," she mumbled between clenched teeth, willing herself not to act like a total scaredy-cat and run behind Niko's back. It took everything she had, until the man stopped not even three feet away from where she near-cowered and smiled.

"Don't worry, miss lady. I'm not going to harm you." He took off his glasses. "Now, the fool standing behind you, on the other hand…"

Confused, Monique looked from the stranger to Niko. He too was smiling. In her calmed state she noted that it was a black running outfit that the man wore, not an outfit meant to keep him from being seen while committing mayhem. Looking back once more, she took in Niko's knee-length running shorts, Nike sneakers and coordinated black T-shirt. Realization dawned. She felt like a dodo. "You know him," she said. Posing the words in a question was unnecessary.

"You might say that. Monique, this is my brother Ike Jr. Ike, this is Monique—excuse me, Mo Slater. She too is running for mayor of Paradise Cove."

Ike Jr. held out his hand. "Running against my brother in his hometown stomping grounds?" Monique stepped away from Niko and shook Ike's hand. "You've got co-jones, woman. I'm impressed."

"It's a pleasure to meet you, Ike. I don't normally scare easily but…"

Niko walked over to where his brother was standing so he could face her. "But what?"

Looking at the two of them next to each other, she was even more embarrassed. Not twins exactly, but they definitely shared the same bloodline. She decided that being honest beat any lie she could tell as she answered his question. "Would you believe…scary movies?"

Niko and Ike looked at each other. "Our mother," they said at once.

"Excuse me?"

Ike responded, "Our mother won't watch anything remotely frightening, and that includes knife-wielding characters in a Saturday-morning cartoon. I once saw her turn away from the Lifetime channel, and this was a movie that was on during daylight!"

"I don't usually watch them, either. But I was visiting someone who loves the ID channel." Ike's stare was blank. Niko shrugged. "Investigation Discovery. It's a channel with shows dedicated to real-life whodunits, murder mysteries and such, with most of the victims I watched today being female and one meeting her demise in surroundings similar to where we now stand. Not exactly the show to watch before deciding on a walk in the woods."

"At the salon, you said you lived in a condo."

"I do."

"The Seventh Heaven complex."

"That's correct."

"Then how did you get in here?" At Monique's cocked brow, Niko held up a hand in defense. "Wait, that may not have come out as I intended. It's just that after an incident here several years ago, the guards really cracked down on who they let beyond the gates, and there is also a patrol that walks the perimeters periodically."

"My godmother lives in Golden Gates."

"Who's your godmother?" Niko asked. Monique told him. "Really? Good old Mrs. Gentry. It's a small world."

Monique chose not to satisfy his obvious curiosity by offering more information. Now that she was calm again, being near him was starting to affect her, and not in a way she liked.

"Listen, guys, I—"

"Nice to meet you, Monique—"

Both she and Ike talked at once. He motioned for her to continue.

"I'll leave you two to your jog and be on my way."

"Oh, no," Ike said. "I was just getting ready to head back to the house. Figured you and Niko could finish the walk together."

"No, really, I—"

"Great idea." Niko reached for her hand. Electricity shot up through it. Monique swore it was a charge with enough voltage to light up Atlantis. The insane way she reacted to him simply had to stop.

She tried to pull away, but he resisted. "See you later, bro. And don't eat all of the strawberry shortcake!"

"No promises!" Ike threw over his shoulder as he began a soft jog away from them.

Both Niko and Monique watched until he rounded a curve. And then it was just the two of them. Alone. In the near darkness. Monique began to shiver and, though there was a slight chill in the air, the weather had nothing to do with it. This time when she pulled her hand away Niko let it go.

"It's late," Monique said, looking at the face of a watch that she couldn't even see. "I really should be going." She took two steps away from him.

"Not like you to run away from a challenge."

She whirled around and took two steps back. "I'm not running away from anything."

"Oh, yeah?" He paused. "You think I don't feel the same thing that you're feeling, the undeniable attraction that's happening between us? Perhaps it's purely physical. Perhaps it's because we're adversaries. Perhaps it's just because we're in close proximity. I don't know. But I felt it last night, when we hugged goodbye. And I felt it just now, when I took your hand." She remained silent. "Are you saying I'm crazy, that you don't feel the energy between us?" He reached for her hand. She jerked it back. "Yes," he said, with a knowing, self-assured grin. "You feel it."

"We're two young, healthy, robust adults," Monique answered, still reeling that Niko had addressed so directly a truth that she'd tried to hide from herself. "It makes sense that we'd be attracted to each other. It happens all the time."

It had never happened before. Not to Monique. Not like this. But she was sure it had happened to other people. That she spoke generally and not specifically was a point she felt didn't need to be shared.

"So you are attracted to me." Monique gave him a look. "Ha! I'm just messing with you, *Mo*. Are you always so serious?" She didn't answer. "We're not in the courtroom, Counselor. You should lighten up a bit." A deep breath but otherwise…nothing. "Shall we walk while talking? I'm headed back to the house, as well."

She nodded. "Okay."

They began walking. "You're a beautiful woman who I'm sure has her share of suitors. Heck, after the way you just reacted upon hearing my brother, maybe stalkers, too. On top of that, you're smart, confident and at the top of your game. I'm sure I'm not the first man who's reacted to what you're working with—a total package."

Actually, he wasn't the first who'd offered her a similar compliment. Rob had said pretty much the same before they'd begun dating. Funny, though, how much sexier it sounded coming from a man like Niko. She found herself wanting to giggle and twirl her hair again.

"I'm sure it's the same for you," she said instead. "In fact, I know it is."

"Oh, really? And how's that?"

"Joy DeWitt. She was more than willing to tell me all about you."

"I'm sure she was."

"I've heard her side. What's your story?"

"I dated her daughter, Ashley. It didn't work out. Then Joy had the nerve to hit on me. I had a few choice words for her about that move."

"Wow. No wonder she detests you."

"I've lost no love for her, either. But Ashley and I are cool. It's a small town. We've got to get along."

"The debate at the salon was rather fun. Unlike the last result, this time you almost won."

"Are you going to keep bringing that up? You know it took me weeks to get over it."

"I understand. It was for the national championship."

"And lifetime bragging rights."

"That, too." They laughed. "I could tell you were upset."

"I'm not used to losing." He looked at her in a way that suggested he was no longer talking about a past meeting.

"Neither am I." The tone in her voice made it clear what she was talking about: the mayoral race.

They continued the short distance to the opening in the community that led to the path, mostly enjoying a companionable silence. Niko was dealing with the surprise of how intriguing he found the woman walking beside him and how attracted he was to her.

Monique was naughtily wondering about Niko's nether anatomy and realizing that never in life had she enjoyed the sexual escapades that others bragged about. Her love life had been fairly constant but average, no bells and whistles or chandelier swinging of which to speak. She felt that given a chance with Niko, the experience would be quite different.

They said their goodbyes.

Monique reached her car and left the confines of the Golden Gates community. She also made up her mind to leave thoughts of anything romantic happening with Niko behind that gilded fence.

Niko walked to his parents' home determined to stay focused, to keep his eyes on the mayoral prize. There was no time to dally with an opponent, no matter how sexy.

Both would learn that what one thought would happen and what sometimes actually occurred were two different things.

Chapter 9

The following Monday, Monique walked into a campaign office already bustling with activity. There were people manning the phone bank, volunteers sitting at a small conference table folding flyers to be mailed, some putting together placards for placement around town and others sifting through clothing for an upcoming career day for homeless and unemployed women. Her campaign manager was in the midst of it all.

"Good morning, Lance."

"Morning, Mo."

"Come into the office."

"Sure."

"Close the door."

He did.

"We've got a busy week ahead." She bypassed her desk and continued on to the large whiteboard positioned against the office's back wall. It was outlined in an at-a-glance format covering the next three months. "Has this been updated?"

"Yes, with several appearances and Memorial Day weekend's Silver Serenade in San Francisco."

"Perfect." Monique's private line on the office phone rang. She looked at the caller ID.

Lance stood. "Do I need to get that?"

"It's Devante. I'll call him back."

"Is he attending the serenade?" Humor laced the question.

"Unless they can play a hip-hop beat with violin and harp, I don't think he'd be interested."

"Sounds like it's going to be a grand affair. My husband and I would love to go." With no response, he added, "Uh, that's a hint, Mo."

"I'd love to take the both of you, but Rob is escorting me."

"Your ex?"

"That's correct."

"You two are still friends? That doesn't happen often."

"You're right. But Rob isn't your average guy."

"He's an above-average type."

"That's right."

"Then why'd you break up with him?"

"Because while we work well as friends, we didn't as romantic partners. Now, enough Q & A on that subject. Let's get back to work.

"We've got dinner with the chamber tonight. I'll be in San Francisco tomorrow and possibly Wednesday if I can't get all of the business handled in one meeting. It looks like Thursday's open?"

"Thought you might need a day in the office."

"Half a day should be enough. Let's see if we can squeeze in the hospital visit that we discussed. See if the administrator is available. I'd like to pick her brain for what we need to consider when planning to build an urgent-care medical facility."

Lance nodded while taking notes on his iPad. "What about the weekend? I can scour the paper for events going on."

"Sure, do that. But keep Friday night open. It's Rob's birthday."

"Just friends, huh?" Lance mumbled under his breath.

"I heard that, and yes…we're just friends. Hold my calls for the next hour. I'm going to work on the speech for tonight."

Monique sat at her desk, and while she'd swear that mere moments had gone by, she looked up and it was four o'clock. Was it really three hours ago that Lance had stuck his head in the door and offered lunch? Her growling stomach was the answer. But it had been like this since her college days. When she got her head involved in something, it was like the rest of the world and everything connected to it faded to the background. Even eating. But not wanting to devour the meal at the chamber meeting like a woman starved, Monique stood, reached for her purse and decided to call it a day.

Two and a half hours later Monique felt revived. She'd stopped by the deli near where her campaign office was housed and, after discovering that it was the owner making her spinach salad, made a pitch for her company's vote, as well. Finding out that the woman would also be at the chamber meeting had been an added plus. Then she'd gone home, squeezed in thirty minutes of yoga, took a hot shower and dressed in her favorite black power suit. Given the admiring looks from the two gentlemen standing just outside of the city auditorium where the dinner was being held, she'd succeeded in appearing professional and a tad bit alluring at the same time.

Squaring her shoulders and placing a pleasant smile on her face, Monique entered the building. She immediately began shaking hands, introducing herself and, thanks to a Dale Carnegie course on memory, addressed those she'd previously met by name. A quick scan around the room told her there were around eighty people in attendance, including the woman who owned the deli. She made her way over to that side of the room.

"Monique!" The cheery, slightly chubby woman with a cute face, gorgeous, naturally auburn hair and sparkly green eyes turned to greet her. "I see you made it."

"And in a much more agreeable mood than I would have been in had I not eaten that salad. It was delicious, by the way. I loved the addition of green apples. Completely unexpected."

"We try," Kari replied with a satisfied shrug. "I'm glad you liked it. The apples were actually my daughter's idea."

"Does she work with you?"

"When she's not away at school. She's a freshman at San Francisco State."

"Excellent. What is her major?"

"She tells me early childhood development, but I say it's parties and boys."

Monique chuckled. "While pursuing a degree, I took that course a time or two. Is she your only child?"

"No. I have three more, a daughter who's sixteen and two boys, twelve and ten."

"You know, Kari, women like you and families like yours are exactly who I had in mind while creating my business-development platform. Particularly businesses ran by women. I want you to have the money you need to improve and expand, to reward good ideas and hard work. And to be able to take care of your family."

"That's all most of us around here want. My husband does well as an over-the-road truck driver, but more attention paid to this level of the working class is always appreciated. I checked out your website after you left. A background as a defense attorney? I wasn't expecting that."

"Yes, well, I've taken a break from defending accused

criminals to defend the future of Paradise Cove for residents like you."

"Oh, she's good," one of the women with whom Kari had been talking said, turning to join the conversation.

"Hello. I'm Mo Slater and I'd like to be your mayor."

"Hi, I...think I've died and gone to heaven."

Monique followed the woman's gaze to see what had so thoroughly gotten her attention. She looked just in time to see four distinguished gentlemen entering the room. Her eyes were immediately drawn to one in particular. Niko nodded, then turned to greet the chamber members who gathered around the foursome as if they were stars.

Of course he'd be here. Why would you think otherwise? The truth was that she'd been so focused throughout the course of her day that she hadn't given it any thought at all. She tried to continue working the room: shaking hands and smiling, networking and hobnobbing, as if Niko's mere presence in the same room didn't sorely affect her. It did.

She meant to ignore him, but occasionally, when in her direct line of sight, she observed his easy camaraderie with everyone present, how he seemed to listen intently and how his smile seemed sincere. It was during one of these moments, while surreptitiously peeking, that Niko turned, smiled at her, and then after whispering something to the gentlemen around him, they all began heading her way.

"Mo?"

"Yes, Kari," she said, turning to face the deli owner.

"This is my daughter's childhood friend who helps me run the shop."

Grateful for the temporary diversion, Monique turned fully away from the oncoming tsunami of testosterone walking toward her and greeted the young woman. The whole time, it was as if she could feel Niko staring at her, could imagine him walking over to lay a firm hand on her shoulder, maybe even a tender kiss on her cheek. For someone not known to be fanciful, she was more than chagrined that being around this man made her think of fairy dust, sugarplums and happily-ever-afters. But it did.

"It was nice to meet you."

Monique smiled and nodded, hoping that the woman hadn't asked a question or made a comment needing a response. Because for her, the past several seconds had been like a black hole filled with one face—his—and one word: *Niko*.

"Ms. Slater."

She slowly turned around. "Mr. Drake," she pleasantly replied. "We meet again."

"I have a feeling we'll be meeting quite often between now and November."

Was it her imagination or did the gleam in his eye signify that he was talking about more than the election? And was it just a notion or did she sorely wish that this was true? She turned to the men standing beside him, immediately recognizing Ike Jr., the brother she'd met on the neighborhood trail. The familial connection of the others was apparent at once, as was the fact that they were all as commanding as they were good-looking and used to being the center of attention in any crowd.

Deciding to draw first blood, she said, "Good evening, gentlemen. My name is Mo Slater, and I'd like to be your mayor."

Their reaction was priceless. The older man chuckled. One of the younger ones, a brother, Monique assumed, jabbed Niko in the ribs. The other man smiled at Monique before saying, "As sharp and feisty as she is fine. Niko, looks like you've got your work cut out for you."

Chapter 10

The older man stepped up first. "It's a pleasure to meet you, Ms. Slater. I'm Ike Drake Sr., chief operating officer of Drake Realty Plus."

They shook hands. "Please, call me Mo or Monique."

"Good to see you again, Monique," Ike Jr. said, shaking her hand.

"You too, Ike. Especially in this safe, well-lit environment."

She saw the look that passed between the others but chose not to elaborate.

Niko chose differently. "Ike and I were jogging the trail out back and looked to have scared her to death."

"Oh," the older man responded, eyeing Monique with a look that was pleasant yet unreadable.

"Do all of you work in the family business?"

Ike Jr. was the first to respond. "In one way or another, except our mom, who rules the roost at home. I'm the president of Drake Realty Plus."

"Hello, Monique. I'm Warren. In addition to being a director at the realty company, I own and operate Drake Ranch and Vineyards."

Monique's eyes shone. "Ah, so yours is the vineyard for whom my dear friend Margo Gentry sang praises. I had the good fortune of trying some of your wine this past weekend. It's wonderful to have such a quality drink that is locally produced."

"Honestly, we can't take all the credit. The grapes are grown locally but then they are trucked to and bottled at Drake Wines and Resort in Temecula, California, owned by our cousins. However, I agree with you. The wine is first-rate."

"I understand you're a powerful L.A. attorney," Ike Sr. said as he eyed her keenly. "What made you leave the bright lights of the big city and come to our small town?"

"What's not to love about Paradise Cove? The name is fitting and the people are lovely. My skill set uniquely qualifies me to help grow what we now have into a vibrant, self-sustaining yet productive component to Northern California's economy. I'm committed to making our business community one that regularly attracts outside visitors. Lastly, I want to make our educational system one of the best in the state, if not the nation."

Niko barely waited for her to finish. "Nice answer, Counselor, but you avoided the question. Why did you leave L.A.?"

She turned to his father. "My job as a defense attorney is satisfying yet stressful. A hard-fought case that took three years to win took its toll. So while I will continue to practice law in some fashion, this was the perfect time for me to take a breath and a break and recharge my batteries by helping others in a different way." She then turned to Niko and cordially asked, "There. How'd I do?"

The look he gave her was unreadable, but it made her quiver inside. Something told her that this man's passion knew no bounds and that whether making love or making war he went all out. She'd stared down shark-finned and bear-clawed prosecutors in the courtroom and never broke a sweat. But under the intense scrutiny of these deep brown eyes she felt vulnerable, almost naked, as though he could peer into her soul. As if the fact that she found him incredibly sexy and superattractive was written on her face. It was mere seconds that he looked at her, but it seemed as though time stood still and the room faded away, save for the man in front of her. Her reaction to him was continually unnerving. Monique wasn't easily fazed and had never been the type of woman to swoon over a man. So why did she feel as if she was about to pass out now?

She was saved from having to ponder further when one of the organizers approached them. "If we can have everyone take their seats, we're going to begin the speeches shortly after the salad course. Mr. Gao is up first, right after the welcome speech by our president and a few words from Mayor Bachman. Ms. Slater, you'll speak next, followed by you, Mr. Drake."

"What about Dick?" Niko asked.

Monique wondered the same thing. She'd read up on both candidates but had yet to personally meet them.

"Dick has a prior engagement and if he makes it here in time will be offering his campaign message at the end of the evening. Now, if you'll follow me you'll see your names, on table one for you, Ms. Slater. Niko—excuse me, Mr. Drake, you and your family are at table two."

As the soup was ladled and the salad consumed, the mayoral candidates made their case for being elected. Monique felt confident about her platform but was admittedly taken by the Drake dynasty. After seeing four of these men in action, she couldn't call their family anything but that. The father, Ike Drake Sr., had a debonair quality and naturally exuded a confident charm. His salt-and-pepper hair was close-cropped and his neatly trimmed goatee gave an air of sophistication that his eloquent conversation about Drake Realty—a conversation Monique heard following the dinner—only emphasized. Warren oozed a good-old-boy quality that made him easily approachable, while Ike Jr., who Monique assumed was the eldest child, seemed like a chip off the old block who had embodied all of the best qualities of all of his elders. Niko was all of these things and more, wrapped in lickable chocolate.

The evening ended just over two hours after it had begun. She was making her way out of the auditorium when the sound of sirens pierced the space. Everyone near her turned in the direction of the blare. They watched as a farmer decked out in a plaid shirt and overalls rushed up the walk.

"Where's the mayor?"

"Inside," the man standing next to Monique responded. "What's going on?"

"Fire at the school," the farmer replied. "I drove by, saw the flames and called 9-1-1. Explosion is what I'm hearing. It looks real bad."

Monique looked around at the worried faces, unaware that her countenance looked even more troubled. "Which school?" she asked, hoping against hope that it wasn't the one she feared.

"Elementary." The farmer pushed past her and walked to the mayor, who rushed out of the auditorium in search of news.

Monique's heart dropped. Without another thought, she raced to the parking lot.

Niko, who'd been watching her while listening to the farmer talk to the mayor, was hot on her heels. "Monique!" She didn't slow down, so he broke into a trot to catch up with her.

"Where are you going?" he asked once he'd reached her and placed a firm hand on her elbow to slow her pace.

"The school." She broke free from his grasp, pointed her remote at her car and unlocked its doors.

Again, Niko reached her. "Wait!" He placed a hand on the open door so that she could not close it. "Ride with us. We're both too upset to drive."

Monique didn't argue. She didn't want to waste time. "Where's your car?"

"Right here," Niko said, as a black town car pulled beside them.

Niko's dad and brother Ike Jr. were in the front. Niko opened the back door, then stepped aside to let Monique enter first. Even in his panicked state he admired the view, how the well-constructed suit skirt clung to Monique's curves and the toned definition of her shapely calves. He saw a familiar SUV and waved as Warren headed to his ranch. When Monique moved to scoot to the far side of the car, Niko held her close.

"Are you calling Lawrence?" Ike Sr. asked his namesake. Ike Jr. nodded. "He's probably left already, son. I know you're worried but try to stay calm."

The sons agreed. Monique did as well, pulling out her own phone to make a call. She knew why her heart was in her throat but, aside from the obvious loss the fire had caused, wondered why Niko was so worried.

"Who's Lawrence?" she asked.

"A childhood friend," Niko explained. "And the school principal." He looked over as Ike Jr. sighed and once again used his thumb to tap the phone screen. "No answer?"

Ike Jr. shook his head. "Busy signal."

"Every parent who has his number is probably calling," Ike Sr. commented as he turned to look at Ike Jr.

Monique noted that he looked as worried as those he was trying to calm.

"We've all known him for years," he said to Monique

as if reading her mind. "I'm good friends with his father. Lawrence is someone we're all proud of, an upstanding citizen and great dad." He looked out the window. "Everything is going to be all right." By now, Monique assumed, he was trying to convince himself as well as the other riders.

She was trying to persuade herself of something as well—that the shortness of breath and butterflies she was experiencing were from nerves about the fire and not the fact that Niko's strong leg kept brushing against hers, and in the cramped quarters of a full-back seat she couldn't escape the raw male heat emanating from his body or the musky, sensuous smell of his cologne. One whiff of it had conjured up memories of the beauty salon and the first time she'd shared space with him, had revived the amorous feelings that she forced down now as she had the day of their fateful meeting. Trying to force her thoughts back to the potential catastrophe at hand, she rubbed her eyes and took a deep breath to still a heartbeat quickened by Niko's nearness, not knowing that this simple act would only make matters worse. A shaky finger tapped the phone screen.

"Calling someone connected with the school?" he asked her.

She nodded. "My mentee, Devante. He works there. I'm getting voice mail."

"It's late. More than likely, there was no one in the building when the fire started," Niko said, placing his arm around her.

"He's the janitor and works after hours." Her voice was soft, strained, as she fought against the urge to remove his arm from around her shoulders. A part of her knew that in no way should she ever feel any part of his anatomy while another part of her wanted to cuddle into his embrace.

Ike Jr. looked at Monique. "Lawrence told me about

him. Said there was a young man working at the school who he'd talked to about becoming a gym teacher. Naturally athletic, great personality and said the kids all looked up to him, especially the boys."

Monique nodded. "That's Devante. Had circumstances been different, he could have played pro sports. He's that talented."

"I sure hope he's all right."

"Me, too." Once again, she dialed the number. This time she left a message. "Devante, this is Monique. Please give me a call as soon as you get this message. There's a fire at the school. I'm worried about you."

They covered the few remaining miles in silence, with Monique battling against thoughts of demise and desire. She didn't know what she'd do if anything happened to the young man she'd decided to mentor and had convinced to come here. Similarly, she didn't know how she'd survive this night, let alone this town, if this strong, relentless desire for the man sitting next to her didn't go away.

Chapter 11

They reached the street where the school was located, now crowded with onlookers watching the firefighters battling the massive blaze. Everyone exited the vehicle. Niko looked over to where two police cars blocked off the part of the street closest to the fire. "There's Randy," he said over his shoulder before walking toward the officers standing beside the patrol cars. He'd known Randy for most of his life. Monique followed closely behind.

"Hey, Officers, Randy." Niko nodded toward the burning building. "That's a nasty blaze."

"Sure is." The officer's eyes remained on a firefighter who'd just opened up another forceful stream of water to combat the flames.

"Any idea how it started?"

Randy shook his head. "Neighbors reported hearing an explosion. But we won't know anything for sure until the fire is out."

"Was anyone inside?"

Randy glanced at Monique, standing beside Niko. "This is Monique Slater," Niko said, having followed his gaze. "She's an attorney from Los Angeles now living here and running for mayor."

"Good to meet you," Monique said, holding out her

hand. "Though I wish it were under different circumstances."

Randy responded with a brief nod before returning his attention to Niko. "Except for one person, it seems that everyone has been accounted for."

Niko and Monique took collective breaths. "Lawrence?" Niko asked.

"Thank God the principal is fine. On his way to an emergency meeting with all of the teachers, school officials, the police chief and some members of the city council. Even if part of the building can be salvaged, we're going to have to move classes to an alternate location temporarily. More than likely that will be the city auditorium."

Monique stepped forward. "Who have you not located?"

"A young man who cleans the place at night."

"Devante?"

"I don't have a name, ma'am, but he's the janitor there."

The news hit like a physical blow. She sagged against Niko. His arm immediately came around her.

"Try him again."

She did, her hands shaking as she made the call.

"No answer?" She shook her head. "Leave another message. He'll call."

"I hope you're right," she replied, regaining her composure and stepping away from his touch.

Niko looked around to see where his brother and father had gone. They were standing with a group of parents, two of whom he knew from their gated community. When he saw the fire chief walking in their direction, he turned to Monique. "Wait here. I'll be right back."

"It looks as though the fire started somewhere near the gymnasium," the chief was saying when Niko reached him. "The whole place has no doubt received smoke damage. Most likely the gym, cafeteria and surrounding class-rooms are totally destroyed."

One of the women listening held up her hand. "But the building was empty, correct? All of our children are safe?"

"We're still trying to account for one employee who so far has not been located. We're hopeful that if he was in the building, he had time to escape before the fire got out of hand."

"You'd think if he escaped that he'd call someone," the woman's husband said. "He has to know the school was looking for him and would be worried."

The woman nodded at her husband before saying to no one in particular, "No one could have survived the blaze in that part of the building."

Niko felt a hand grab his arm and knew that Monique had not followed his instruction. He turned to see her eyes wide with fear.

"They found him?"

"No," Niko said, gently guiding her away from the group. "The chief said that they wouldn't be able to check the building until tomorrow, once the fire is out and the scene has cooled enough for a thorough search."

Monique brought a hand to her mouth as she shut her eyes against unexpected tears. "I asked him to come here," she said, forcing down anguish and squaring her shoulders in an effort to regain control of her emotions. "I swore that by leaving the city he'd be safe."

Niko almost reached for her, but remembering her re-action from earlier, he refrained. "Why don't you come over to my house, share a cup of tea? My dad is friends with the fire chief. I can make sure we're notified as soon as there's news."

"But you just said it would be morning before a thor-ough search is conducted."

"Yes, but a preliminary one might be done tonight. I'd feel better knowing that you're not home alone, worrying yourself to death. If we haven't heard something by midnight I can have my driver take you home."

"That's not necessary. I've handled my share of crises."

"Then will you come and sit with me until I calm my nerves?"

Monique eyed him speculatively. "I don't know if that's a good idea."

"Why not?"

She looked around. "This is a very small town. I don't want someone to see me go into your house and start tongues wagging."

"I wouldn't worry about it. But if you're truly concerned, I'll drop Ike and Dad off and drive the town car. It has tinted windows and I'll pull into the garage."

"Hmm. Sounds like an action you've done before."

"Join me at my home and I'll tell you about it."

"Oh, wait. My car…"

"I'll make sure it's parked in your driveway before 6:00 a.m. Anything else?"

"You really don't have to do this, you know. I am worried about Devante, but I'll be fine."

"I know. You're a strong, proud woman with an *S* on your cape. I know a few of those, not the least of whom is my mother." He was glad for the small smile this comment elicited. "So humor me. Come over and share a cup of tea."

"Is that all you're interested in sharing?"

The frank question elicited a raised brow. His intentions when he'd asked Monique over had been totally honorable, but her innocent query opened his mind to other possibilities. The image of her lush backside and shapely legs as she'd entered the car came instantly to mind, as did what he could do ensconced between said shapely legs. Why he was so concerned about her welfare, even to the point of feeling somewhat responsible for her well-being, was another question he'd have to figure out. But that would have to happen later. Right now, he wanted to get away from this scene and the mixture of curious and admiring eyes that were starting to be aimed in his direction. Then he saw Ashley walking toward them, staring hard at Monique. It was definitely time to leave.

"Let's head to the car," he said to Monique as he pulled out his phone. He dialed his father's number, careful to maintain a respectful distance between him and his rival when for whatever unfathomable reason all he wanted to do was wrap her in his arms. "You about ready, Dad?" He listened to the response. "Okay. Let me know as soon as you hear anything." He ended the call. "Dad and Ike are going to stay a little longer. They'll ride back with one of the neighbors."

"Niko, maybe I should—"

"Let someone take care of you? Yes, I agree." His voice was firm and final, the statement delivered in a tone that brooked no argument, even from a nationally recognized defense attorney who'd once kicked his butt in a college debate.

They reached the car and rode the ten minutes from the school to Golden Gates in silence. Monique had passed on rolling low in the backseat, but once they'd reached the home, Niko pulled into the garage.

"I'm going to great lengths to ensure you're not associated with me."

Monique laughed and opened her door.

A slight frown marred Niko's handsome countenance as he watched her. "Why do I get the feeling you're enjoying a private joke."

"I am."

Her look was soft and playful, and Niko discovered he quite liked it. Usually, it was the cool, professional demeanor that was brought to the fore. They reached the door that led from the garage to the hallway beyond it. Niko opened the door. "Care to share?"

Monique stepped inside. "I can't believe this is your home." They continued walking down a hall with a laundry room on one side and a mudroom on the other before spilling into a larger area where the kitchen, dining room and great room were visible.

"Really, why?"

"Because shortly after moving here, Margo gave me a tour of the neighborhood. I said this was one of my favorite houses. Remembering back, she didn't comment. That's what I find humorous. Now I know why."

"She didn't want you to know that you were admiring the home of your stiffest competition?"

Monique had been thinking of her competition's potential stiffness all night. Now that she was in the privacy of his residence, she'd have to work harder than ever—pun intended—to keep her thoughts PG.

"Sometimes it's hard to know exactly what Margo is thinking. She's quite the character. But my comment stands. You have a very nice home."

Built by Drake Realty a little over five years ago, Niko's home was large yet tasteful, opulent but in an understated sort of way. Pristine landscaping included large trees and bushes and obscured much of the actual home from the street. Visitors were always surprised to come in and find it was so large. Monique was no exception.

"I never would have guessed you had so much room. Do you mind my asking the square footage?"

"Not at all. It's three thousand square feet, not including the outdoor living space. More than enough for a home of one. Too much sometimes." As she continued to look around with genuine interest, he added, "Would you like a tour?"

"If you don't mind."

After giving a quick description of why he'd chosen the muted colors and fabrics for the rooms visible from where they were standing, he led her to floor-to-ceiling glass doors that led to a flawlessly designed outdoor space that included a living area with couches, chairs and a fire pit, a full stainless-steel kitchen with colorful stone bar, a nice-size pool and similarly designed spa. The same colors that dominated inside—a mixture of tan, gray, cream and black—continued outside. Luscious plants and vibrant pillows warmed the scene, and the design of the privacy fence made it less offensive to the eye. All in all, Monique loved it and was surprised to note that had she designed it herself very little would change. She loved the clean lines and thoughtful layout, and Niko's home office rivaled that which she had on L.A.'s Sunset Boulevard.

The upstairs tour was blessedly brief. She felt hot just stepping foot inside his spacious master suite. She looked at the custom-made bed, with its unique blend of ebony wood and stainless steel covered with a cozy-looking comforter Niko said was a blend of cotton and raw silk, and imagined him sprawled against it. Ignoring the smirk she saw upon her declining to check out the master bath and closet, they made quick work of the remaining upstairs rooms, which included a state-of-the-art gym, and returned to the kitchen.

Monique thanked him for the tour. She was impressed, first with the man and now with the understated and elegant home where he resided. It had given her a brief reprieve from worrying about Devante, a thought that returned full force as soon as she sat on one of the bar stools in front of the unique island made of bright recycled glass. Blue, orange and green slivers of glass provided a vibrant splash of color to an otherwise monotone room. She picked up her phone and, when she saw that no calls had been missed, tried reaching him again. There was still no answer and this time the call went straight to voice mail.

"If something has happened to him, I won't be able to forgive myself."

"Come on, now. Don't think like that. You've got to stay positive. Try to relax."

She took a deep breath, leaned against the chair back and watched how comfortable Niko appeared in the kitchen. He'd put on water to boil, set a container of various teas in front of her and was now placing slices of lemon onto a plate. Their eyes met, and a familiar warmth traveled to its usual places. She was sure she was blushing and prayed the lighting kept this fact a secret. As for the desire that made her clutch her thighs together, she thanked the island for keeping hidden the lower half of her anatomy.

He turned from an open cabinet. "Sugar or honey for your sweetener?"

Neither, Monique was sorely tempted to say. The dark caramel making her heart patter and mouth water couldn't be found in the pantry. To see it, Niko would have to look in a mirror.

Chapter 12

"Monique? Your choice of tea?"

She hadn't realized she'd been daydreaming. About Niko. Again. She reached for the first bag in the container, an herbal blend infused with citrus and spice. "Sorry."

"I know you want to hear from him."

"Actually, what I want is right in front of me." She handed Niko the tea bag. "This sounds good."

"One of my favorites." Niko opened the cellophane packet and placed the tea bag in an oversize mug bearing the Drake Realty logo. He opened another packet and placed it in the same type of mug before turning off the now whistling teapot and covering the bags with boiling water. Then he reached for cup covers to let the tea steep, before taking a seat across from her. Seeing the frown on her face, he softly said, "Tell me about Devante."

"He's basically a good person, though no stranger to the system, mostly in for petty theft. One involved a gun. That upped the charge to armed robbery, a felony. They wanted to try him as an adult. I researched his backstory and was quite moved. He was your stereotypical inner-city child statistic. Father in prison whom he'd never met, mother on drugs, eldest child strapped with the responsibility of raising his younger siblings. That's why he stole. It was either that or starve. I successfully argued that his case be kept in juvenile court and from that point on took him under my wing as a mentee."

"Becoming so involved with a client? That's risky business."

If you only knew, Monique thought before quickly shoving the unfortunate memory to the back of her mind. Way back. "I've no regrets," she finally replied. "Unless I hear that he didn't survive the fire."

Again, Niko felt the almost overwhelming desire to take care of Monique, to protect her and erase the worry lines from her face. He'd spent most of his life surrounded by beautiful, strong women and wondered at this pull that she had on his heartstrings. He reasoned that maybe it was because as an attorney himself, he knew how hard it could be for a woman in this field. She couldn't have survived without a knock or two. Or maybe it was the fact that as strong and powerful as she appeared, there was a vulnerability and sensitivity about her that shone in her eyes. When she heard about the fire or talked about Devante, for instance. And speaking of fire, she'd tried to hide it, but he'd detected the flame of desire in her eyes when she looked at him. She'd said it was only natural that two healthy adults such as themselves be attracted to each other. Would she be willing to have said it was natural for two healthy adults to act on such attraction?

He looked over to see that she'd averted her face. *Is she crying?* Instinctively, he walked over to where she sat and placed his arms around her. "It's going to be all right, Monique."

He felt her shoulders heave and thought she'd pull away. Like all the other times. But she didn't. She leaned into him and placed her arms around his waist. He pulled her closer to him and began rubbing his hand across her back. "It's okay, sweetheart. You can let go. We're all very concerned. Everything is going to be all right." He brushed his lips across her temple and kissed her there.

She stilled. Her arms around him loosened slightly. Niko silently chided himself. He hadn't meant to kiss her. It was a reflex, pure and simple. She pulled back. He lifted his head, ready to apologize. Until he saw the look in her eyes and how they quickly shifted from looking into his eyes to looking at his lips. Just before she leaned in and joined hers to them. She did this, but moved no further. So Niko took over. He slowly moved his head, rubbing his lips across hers, creating a delicious friction that immediately increased the heat. Her mouth opened and it took all of his restraint not to plunder her sweetness like a love-starved youth. But she didn't need that type of treatment right now. She needed gentleness and kindness and understanding. He was there to give it all.

Using his tongue, he outlined her lips, still not delving inside. Instead he kissed her closed eyelids, kissed each cheek before finding her mouth once again. This time, when she opened it, he slowly, gently, slid his tongue inside, flicking it against hers even as he repositioned his head to kiss her more fully. He continued—deeper yet tenderly—lightly massaging her back as their tongues introduced themselves and got to know each other, as one hand lowered to her hips while the other found the nape of her neck to take the kiss deeper still. As he stroked her mouth with his tongue he felt her hands tighten, felt her fingernails scrape across his shirt's cotton fabric. The act was filled with both wanting and restraint. She shivered, and he felt her nipples harden even as his shaft followed suit. His hand moved from her hip around to that pebbled hardness, giving the nipple a light squeeze before continuing to run his finger lightly across it. Somewhere in the recesses of his mind came the thought that he should end this tantalizing kiss; that now was not the time or place for seduction.

After another moment of some of the sweetest sugar he'd ever tasted, he reluctantly pulled away. Without conscience she leaned forward, trying to reconnect with her current single source of joy.

"Monique."

She opened her eyes and it was as though she were awakening from a dream. He noticed the second she came to herself and realized what had just occurred. She dropped her head and straightened her blouse.

"I'm sorry," he said, immediately putting the blame on himself. "I got carried away."

"It's what I wanted," Monique replied. She took a deep breath, looked him square in the eyes. "It's what I want now."

"I know. I want to kiss you in ways you've never imagined and love away every ounce of anxiety you're feeling right now. But I won't do that. Not tonight, when you're worried and vulnerable, seeking relief from those feelings." He placed a gentle hand under her chin. "When we make love, it will be because you want me to give you something to remember, not because of problems that you're trying to forget."

Monique stood. "Now it's my turn to apologize. Kissing you—no matter how good it felt—was inappropriate. Worrying about Devante has obviously got me acting out of character. Especially since…"

"Since what?"

"Never mind." She stood. "This wasn't a good idea. I should go home, try to get some sleep if I can."

"Do you really think that's possible? Sleep, that is?"

"I don't know, but I need to be where I can think."

"And that can't happen around me?"

She eyed him closely and noted his question was genuine; no superciliousness or sarcasm anywhere.

"No, quite frankly. You're right. I'm vulnerable and in this state capable of making mistakes based on bad judgment."

"Are you speaking from experience?"

"Yes."

"Want to talk about it? We can move to the living room or dining room. I'll sit on my side and promise to behave."

She sat back at the island. He reheated the water. His ordinary actions soothed her. She was still worried, but more relaxed. After fixing their cups of tea, the two moved to the living room. Silence descended as each sipped tea and scanned thoughts. The quiet could have been awkward, but it wasn't. For Monique it was comforting. She was glad she'd stayed when moments ago she'd wanted to run, not only away from Niko, but from uncomfortable memories.

This situation with Devante brought back an unfortunate incident that she'd managed to put behind her. Images flashed and feelings resurfaced. Another time when she'd tried to help a client and things hadn't gone so well. She'd lost control and made an unfortunate decision. Right intention. Wrong execution. Could what she tried to do with Devante prove another bad move?

"Have you ever dated a client?" She looked up, surprised that the words she'd been thinking had actually been spoken aloud. She hadn't meant for them to be; only a handful of people knew why she'd ask.

"Interesting question. I did, once. Have you?"

She looked at him. "I did, once."

Maybe it was the cushy chair, maybe the tea; maybe it was her worry about Devante, the fire and all that had happened tonight. Then again, maybe it was the kiss, and the innate knowledge that what had gotten started tonight would one day be finished. But Monique found herself opening up to the man who was her adversary and sharing something that she swore would never be told again.

Chapter 13

"I was fresh out of law school," Monique began, tracing the rim of the teacup with her thumb, "working in my first firm. He was our client, facing ten years for money laundering. It was the first time I'd been around…someone like him. I thought I'd be repulsed, thought I'd have to work to find compassion for a man I'd assumed was just a no-good lowlife out for who he could con. I was wrong. He was intelligent and funny with tons of charm. He loved reading and current events. He told me that he was innocent. I believed him. We'd talk about what was going on in the world, about his dreams and aspirations, which I was surprised to even find out he had. One thing led to another and…"

His eyes widened.

"No. It didn't go that far. We didn't have sex. But during this revealing conversation there was inappropriate touching." She shrugged her shoulders and looked in Niko's eyes for signs of judgment. She saw none.

"He was convicted and is doing five to ten years in prison. As his attorney, I could speak with him privately. During one of these visits is when things got carried away. Hugging mostly, and we kissed. It shouldn't have happened.

"My boss found out. Because of this inappropriate conduct, I lost my job. Of course that was the right consequence, though it's still painful to recall those dark, early days of my career. My godfather advised me to end all contact. So I wrote him a letter. Short, to the point, about my being fired and therefore being unable to continue to represent him. I'm sure he was devastated to read its contents. After what he'd endured, he believed I was the one person who would never leave him. But I knew it was best to end all contact and walk out of his life."

"That had to be tough, and even more difficult to find another employer."

"Thankfully one of my former teachers had an influential friend in the legal field. The firm he recommended knew my story, but gave me a chance based on my teacher's recommendation. I've worked hard every day to make sure they never regret taking a chance on me."

Niko was silent, watching her, taking it all in. "From what I've read, their gamble paid off."

"So it seems."

"What did your parents say? With their high expectations, they had to be devastated."

"They were disappointed, which increased my shame."

"Do you still love him?"

Now it was Monique's turn to be surprised. Her head shot up, and she stared at Niko to gauge if he was kidding. He was not. "I never said I loved him."

Niko was equally resolute. "Your actions did."

"I wanted so badly for him to succeed. There'd been bad choices but he was a good man. I feel the same way about Devante. He just needs a chance." She drained the rest of her tea and once again reached for her phone to call him. "It's still going to voice mail." Niko nodded but remained silent. "So what about you? How many hearts have you broken?"

He shrugged. "I hope none, but maybe a few."

"Was one of them the woman at the fire?"

"What woman?"

"The woman responsible for us leaving so quickly. I saw her making a beeline to you just before you rushed us away."

"Oh, you saw that, huh?"

"Keen observation is partly what makes me a good attorney. And why they pay me the big bucks."

"That was Joy's daughter, Ashley, the one I told you about the other night." What he didn't share was Ashley's negative impression of Monique or the fact that since seeing them together at the scene of the fire she'd called and texted several times.

"Pretty girl."

"Very, and sometimes full of drama. There's more to making a relationship work than having good looks. Besides, this conversation started with your talking about a client you dated. How did it turn into one about my love life?"

"Turnabout is fair play."

Niko smiled, realizing that he was quite enjoying himself. Not only was it good to see the worry lines alleviated from Monique's face, but it was nice to spar with someone who could obviously hold her own in the verbal exchange. Hanging with Ashley had been physically rewarding, but they had not kept company because of her intellectual range. Thinking back, he couldn't remember a female outside his family whom he'd enjoyed talking to more. *Too bad she's off-limits. Maybe after I win the election...*

"I really should be going," Monique said after looking at her watch.

"They must not have any new information. My dad would have called."

"Then I'll accept a ride to my car. I have an early-morning appointment tomorrow."

"Who with?"

"Seriously? You think I'm going to show my hand to the enemy camp?" A wisp of a smile took the sting from her comment.

"If you don't mind, I'll have my driver return you." He rang him and then walked with her toward the hallway leading to the garage. "I have enjoyed your company this evening. It's going to be hard to administer this severe political beating to you, but they say all's fair in love and politics."

"That's something that you should remember in November, when you're rubbing that sorely defeated behind."

"Ha!"

They became silent as they reached the door. "Thanks for this interlude. I'm a lot calmer now."

"Anytime."

"In my earlier vulnerable state, I shared some things that I hadn't planned to. I know we're in what's sure to become a highly contested race but—"

"Shh." Niko silenced her with a chaste kiss. "Don't even worry about it. What was discussed in my home will stay here."

He hugged her. She hugged him back. He wanted to kiss her again. Would have, but he heard the garage door opening. "Are you sure you don't want to just be taken home? We can make sure your car is delivered by morning."

"No. I'd really like to pick it up tonight. Thanks again, for everything. Let me know the moment your father has any news."

Niko nodded. "Call me when you hear from Devante."

Monique smiled and, fighting the urge to join her lips with his, hurried to get into the town car.

Niko stepped out into the garage, hidden by its darkness. He wasn't sure whether or not she could see him but waved anyway. Stepping back into his home, he was assailed by a sense of loneliness. He was also keenly aware that having lived in the house for years and waved away many a female from its confines, this was the first time one had left him feeling bereft. Later, sleep eluded him. He tossed and turned with images of Monique and what they would have done had she spent the night. Finally, about an hour later, sleep finally came. And so did Monique…in his dreams.

Chapter 14

Monique reached the city-auditorium parking lot and her car, which aside from the city vehicles was the only one there. After thanking the driver, who refused to take a tip, she got into her vehicle and headed home. With all of the thoughts swirling in her mind, she was thankful for the quiet time. Now that she'd been alone with him, there was no doubt in her mind that the lust she felt for Niko could easily turn into love. He was handsome, thoughtful, successful and smart. What woman couldn't fall head over heels for a man like him? And those kisses? Good Lord! He hadn't forced the situation. It was what she'd wanted. Now she wanted much, much more.

"If only…" she whispered, as she turned the corner and took in the desolate streets. Paradise Cove was a lovely town—peaceful, beautiful and nearly crime-free. Her thoughts moved to the fire and its cause. The fire chief had offered nothing tonight and that was understandable. But experience had taught Monique to be suspicious at least and skeptical at best. That way you were left with few surprises. With a heave of her shoulders she sighed and thought of Devante. At the same exact time, her phone rang.

She looked at the caller ID. Devante!

She pressed the button on the steering wheel, gripping it

for whatever news would be delivered when she answered. "My God, Devante. I've been so worried!"

"I'm sorry," a cautious-sounding voice answered. "My phone died. I just started charging it and saw the missed calls."

"Did you listen to my message?"

"About the fire? Yeah, I heard it. Sorry you were worrying about me, but I wasn't there tonight."

"You were off tonight? Why didn't the school officials inform the fire department?"

"Aw, man, you're going to be upset with me. But I tried to call you earlier today. You were in a meeting."

Monique remembered the call she'd declined while speaking with Lance. "Yes, right. You did call. To say what?"

"See, I sorta got caught up in a situation and wasn't able to make it to work by my start time. I was going to make up the hours, just go in later, that's all."

"And you didn't call the school and say you'd be late?"

"My boss is cool like that. He knows I do good work, so he doesn't trip on what time I get there."

Having already gone from worry to anger, Monique's ire went up a notch. "So what is this situation that had you so caught up that your phone died, and you couldn't recharge it until two in the morning?"

"Ah, Mo…"

"Don't 'ah, Mo' me. I've been worried sick! Where were you?"

A loud sigh came through the speakers. "I was over at my girl's house. She lives about a half hour from P.C. We fell asleep and whatnot, and when I woke up late, I figured I'd just get to the school whenever I got there and do my thing, you know? Like I said, I was going to put in the same hours, just a little later than usual. We heard about the fire on the news, but I didn't know y'all were looking for me. I apologize, Monique. You're one of the few who believes in me. I know you always have my best interest at heart and I'm sorry to have kept you up worrying about me."

"I accept your apology," she said, after a pause. "Have you called the police or the fire department?"

"Why would I do that?"

Again, Monique tamped down her ire. Someone of Devante's background had little use for law enforcement. "Never mind. I'll let them know you've been found so they don't spend any more time looking for you in the rubble."

"Thank you."

Monique turned into her driveway, emotional weariness adding to her physical state. "You're welcome. I'll talk to you later."

The next morning, Monique sat at her table sipping a cup of tea. She'd been going through the motions of checking her email, but in actuality she'd been thinking about Niko and replaying their time together last night in her mind. Having had a fitful night's sleep, she'd finally gotten up at six-thirty, put in a couple of loads of laundry and then settled down for a half-hour phone conversation with her mother. Five minutes in and as much as she loved her mother, she'd regretted making the call.

"Good morning, Mom."

"Morning, Monique. You're up early. Busy day ahead?"

"No rest for the weary."

"Or, it seems, for those campaigning for public office. I hope you're taking care of yourself."

"I am," Monique said around a yawn.

"Perhaps you should have gone to bed earlier."

"There was a fire here last night at Paradise Cove Elementary."

"Oh, no."

"Yes." She shared what she knew with her mother. "Fortunately no one was killed or injured. But the damage is extensive. I'm sure it will go into the millions of dollars."

"I'm sorry to hear about that and can understand your having to be on the scene. You know I support you, but becoming mayor, even of a small town, will be a huge responsibility. I wish you hadn't broken up with Rob and had a man there to support you."

"The townspeople are all very supportive of each other. I'll be fine."

"Rob loves you, Monique. And he's such a nice man."

"Yes, he is, but the relationship is over and that decision is final."

Monique knew that as far as her mother was concerned, any black man working was a good one. Having married at the tender age of twenty-two, her old-fashioned mother thought Monique an old maid. Her mother had liked Rob from the start, appreciated his Ivy League background and white-collar job. It was probably why she chose to stay in denial and not accept the fact that except for friendship, Rob was in Monique's rearview mirror.

"I sure hope this desire to enter politics doesn't have an adverse effect on your personal life," Mrs. Slater continued. "In the event of your winning, I hope you'll reconsider your decision. Rob would be an excellent partner in your political lifestyle."

"Rob and I will always be good friends. He's visiting this weekend and will join me Memorial Day weekend for a fundraiser in San Francisco."

"That's great to hear! Give him a hug for me."

"I will."

This comment effectively satisfied her mother and they spent the rest of the conversation talking about family and her dad's early-retirement plans. During the call, she received a text from Rob confirming that he'd made his flight reservations. Monique made a mental note to prepare the guest room. She wanted to make sure that Rob understood that this was a platonic visit…not a romantic one.

At the respectable hour of 8:00 a.m., Monique reached for her cell phone and dialed Niko's number. He answered on the first ring. "Good morning."

"Good morning, beautiful. Wait, I can call you *beautiful,* can't I, without fearing a charge of harrassment?"

"I don't know, Counselor. A word like that could be deemed inappropriate use with your equal, right along with ones like *sugar* and *dear.*"

"My apologies."

"I don't hear one ounce of sorry in your voice." Niko had elicited Monique's first true smile of the morning.

"But I've been properly schooled. Good morning, Monique."

"I've got a busy day ahead of me and not long to talk, but I wanted you to know that I heard from Devante."

"Excellent! When?"

"Last night, on my way home."

"And you're just now calling?"

"I thought you might have been asleep and didn't want to wake you."

"See, I told you he was okay. Was he there when the fire started?"

"No, thank God."

"You really have a vested interest in this guy."

"I have a soft heart for those who weren't blessed with the same type of upbringing as you and I."

"An admirable trait, especially for someone running for public office."

"You sound sincere."

"I am. Bryce was right."

"Bryce Clinton, your campaign manager?"

"That is correct."

"Right about what?"

"When he found out you were running, he said I had my work cut out for me." His voice lowered, remaining professional, but barely. "He was definitely right about that."

An incoming call for Niko cut short the conversation. Monique hung up the phone and headed to the campaign office. During the less-than-ten-minute drive, she was keenly aware of two things: speaking with Rob never made her na-na tingle and talking to Niko always did.

Chapter 15

Monique was thankful for the busy week she'd had, although one of the reasons annoyed her. During the fire investigation, some type of accelerant had been discovered, leading them to believe the fire may have been deliberate. They interviewed several people, including Devante. That in itself was not a problem. However, when they not only confirmed his alibi three times but also brought him to the station for further questioning, and then called his parole officer for further discussion, she felt they'd crossed the line. Devante felt he'd been profiled, and she couldn't blame him. Men with prison records were often prejudged. With no job and a bad attitude, and against her orders, Devante had gone back to L.A. She'd spent time she didn't have to track him down and get him placed in a home that met the rules for parolee residents.

The doorbell rang. She looked at her watch. Rob. Her busy week had made her almost forget his visit, as well. "Hey there," she said, opening the door wide so that he could enter, and stepped into his outstretched arms. "Good to see you."

He hugged her as though it had been two years instead of a few months since he'd seen her. "You're a sight for sore eyes." His lips swept against her ear in a manner Monique was sure Rob meant to be sexy. Unfortunately for both of them, instead of heat she felt annoyance, his wet kiss feeling sloppy instead of scintillating, as was his goal.

She stepped back and crossed her arms.

"I'm sorry. Just friends, right?"

"Rob, I'll always care for you, but our being together romantically is over." If he didn't understand this message, her next statement was crystal clear. "Let's take your luggage into the guest room.

"Are you hungry?" she asked, as he begrudgingly passed her master suite on the way to the spare bedroom.

"Yes, but not for dinner."

Ignoring his comment, she replied, "Let's have a glass of wine before heading out. I know you'll love the salmon at Acquired Taste." Without waiting for an answer, she walked out of the bedroom and down the hall.

Rob met her in the kitchen, where she was opening a bottle of chilled chardonnay. He leaned against the refrigerator, crossed his arms and watched her closely. "What's going on with you, Monique?"

Monique took a deep breath, reaching for wineglasses to gather her thoughts before she turned to face him. "The mayor's race is really heating up, and my numbers are growing. It's exciting yet stressful. Even with a campaign manager, the responsibility is huge."

"This is too much for you to be doing alone." Sincerity dripped from Rob's voice. Once again he moved in for a hug. Her look stopped him. "I'd move my practice in a heartbeat. Just say the word."

It was the second time he'd suggested moving to Paradise Cove. She came precariously close to telling him the truth: that the thought of putting distance between them had aided in her decision to relocate in the first place. But she'd already hurt him enough. "I couldn't ask you to do that," she said instead. "If I don't win the mayor's seat, there's no guarantee that I'll even stay in this town. In fact, I'm almost sure I'd return to L.A."

She lifted her glass. "To what shall we toast?"

"To your mayoral victory, of course."

They clinked glasses, then walked into Monique's small but tastefully appointed living room.

Monique sat in one of two accent chairs. "How's business?"

"Steady, growing. I'm planning to hire another accountant for the firm."

"It's a testament to your skills that the company keeps growing, even in an economy that continues to be shaky."

"Thanks, Monique. I appreciate that. Though I'd always envisioned my company expanding with you by my side."

Monique took a sip of wine. There were no words to say. This past week had left her thoughts in shambles. Niko had turned her emotional world upside down, so much so that she had no idea of her personal future. She was certain, however, that it wouldn't conclude with Rob Baldwin. He was a good man, but she couldn't have kept denying her true feelings. Still, the thought of having hurt him made her sad.

Thirty minutes later they walked into Acquired Taste, one of Paradise Cove's two main restaurants. After a short wait they were escorted to a table. Seated at the center of the dining room were some of the finest citizens California had to offer. Holding court was none other than Niko Drake.

He saw her immediately and stood as she walked by the table. "Monique, hello!"

She stopped. "Hello, Niko. Gentlemen."

"Let me introduce my family. You've met Ike Jr. and Warren."

"Yes. Hi, guys."

Various greetings rang out as the men stood.

"These are my cousins from Southern California, Dexter and Donovan Drake."

Dexter and Donovan stood. "A pleasure to meet you," they responded, shaking her hand.

"This is their brother-in-law, my cousin, Jackson Wright, and my brother Terrell."

Jackson and Terrell stood and greeted her. All eyes turned to the man by her side.

"This is Rob Baldwin," she said. "Rob, this is mayoral candidate Niko Drake." Niko turned to shake hands. Even though he was only six feet tall, his solid structure seemed to dwarf Rob's five foot nine.

Monique watched Niko's eyes sweep her body before returning his attention to Rob. "Are you helping Monique with the campaign?"

"You could say that," Rob responded before placing a possessive arm around her waist.

Niko's face remained passive. "I see."

"Good to see you all," Monique quickly interjected. "Have a nice evening." Without waiting for an answer, she deftly removed Rob's hand from her waist and then turned to follow the waiter.

Silence descended like a curtain as soon as they sat down. Much like earlier in her home, Rob eyed her critically. "You seemed nervous back there."

"Did I?" She reached for the water glass, gripping it firmly.

He noticed. "And now."

"*Annoyed* is probably a better word. You purposely tried to give the impression that there was more between us than friendship. I'd like us to remain cordial, Rob. But if you continue to try to force a relationship where one no longer exists, then I'll have no choice but to cut ties with you altogether."

"I apologize," Rob answered after a lengthy pause. "It was a natural reaction after seeing how he looked at you."

"Who?"

"Niko. It was definitely not as an adversary. Is there something going on with you two?"

"Rob, if we're going to enjoy this weekend together, and I hope we will, I think we should change the direction of this conversation."

Another pause. Rob conceded. "Whatever."

Their salads arrived, and Rob and Monique successfully steered the conversation to less volatile topics: climate change, politics and their mutual love of classical music that had them looking forward to the Silver Serenade. Monique breathed a sigh of relief when halfway through their entrée she saw the Drake men get up and leave. Normally bypassing dessert for health reasons, she indulged in the apple pie à la mode just to avoid the inevitable—going back to her home with Rob.

But finally, it had to happen. The ride home was quiet, the tension intense. They dressed for bed. "I'm going to turn in," she said once they'd shared small talk and watched both the local and national news. "Towels and toiletries are in the bathroom cabinet. There's juice, water and snacks in the fridge. Make yourself at home. Good night." She rose from the couch.

"Monique?"

"Yes?"

"I'm sorry for how I acted earlier after meeting Niko. We've been apart for months, but in my heart, you're still my lady. It's hard to adjust to being just your friend."

"It is a big change, but also a necessary one."

Neither of them realized it, but even bigger changes were just down the road.

Chapter 16

The weekend was over. It was Monday morning, and Monique was in bed. She felt horrible, and a low-grade fever, sore throat and pounding headache were only part of the reason. The other ailment was Rob and the fight they'd had that had sent him packing—literally.

For his birthday on Saturday, they'd spent the day hiking, then had a catered dinner with Margo and some of her friends. Everyone had laughed and had a good time. Yesterday, the morning had started off great, as well. They'd gone for a power walk and then to the Cove Café for breakfast. She'd taken him to her office and shown him around town, driven him over to the burned-out school. But while sitting on the couch and watching a movie, Rob had once again tried to get romantic.

She'd opened her mouth before thinking. Truth spilled out. "Will you please stop? We've been through this a dozen times. I don't want to be intimate with you, ever, okay?"

The hurt in his eyes brought instant regret. "I didn't mean to say it that way. I—"

"It's him, isn't it?" Rob had sneered. "I bet you find Niko attractive."

"Rob, I don't want to hurt you."

"Too late for that."

"You're a good man…"

"But I'm not Niko Drake."

"He has nothing to do with this conversation."

"He has everything to do with it!" When she didn't respond, he said, "Look me in the eye and tell me that you don't have feelings for him. Don't lie. Be honest."

Five seconds went by. And then five more.

He crossed his arms. "I'm waiting."

She sighed. "It doesn't matter how I feel about him, Rob. He and I are opponents in a political race. Nothing can happen between us."

"But you want it to."

"It doesn't matter what I want."

"I have my answer."

He'd swept by her then, snatched his carry-on from the closet, slammed it on the bed and began throwing his clothes inside.

She'd followed him. "Please, Rob. Don't leave angry. We've been friends for so many years."

"I thought I could handle it. But the truth of the matter is I don't want to be just another friend." He stomped into the bathroom and removed his toiletry bag. Tossing it on top of the clothes, he shut the case, zipped it and placed it on the ground. "I wanted to be your husband. I wanted to see your eyes light up when you saw me the way they did when you saw Niko." She would have objected but he put up his hand. "Don't deny it," he said, his voice soft, all fight gone. "I know what I saw. Men like him are always the ones desired. And women like you who desire them always get hurt."

"What does that mean?" He left the room. She trailed after him as he walked to the door.

When he reached it he turned to her. "You'll find out."

She'd called and left messages. They weren't returned.

In hurt and anger was not how she'd wanted Rob to leave her life.

Her phone rang. She pushed the speakerphone button. "Good morning."

"Is it really?" Lance asked. "You sound horrible."

"Thanks a lot."

"We don't have any appearances or meetings today. Why don't you take advantage of the light schedule and get some rest?"

"I think I will. Send over any emails that are important. I'm going to work from home."

Monique pulled herself out of bed, grabbed her robe and the laptop and headed downstairs. She put on water for tea and fired up her computer. There was only one problem. She didn't feel like working.

"What do people do when stuck at home?" she mumbled to the empty room. Eyeing the remote, she picked it up and turned on the TV. She flipped past a couple of major networks before settling on the community station, which featured news of Paradise Cove. After less than two minutes, a familiar face came on the screen: Niko's. A voiceover spoke while various images of him flashed: handling business, talking to farmers, laughing with a group of women, riding a horse.

Geez, he makes as good a cowboy as he does a businessman.

Turning up the volume, she listened. "…along with his family at Drake Realty Plus, has created over fifty new jobs in the construction industry. And every holiday season their turkey-and-trimmings giveaway helps families in need. For over fifty years, in Paradise Cove the Drake name has been synonymous with helping people and making progress. As your mayor, Niko Drake plans to continue this legacy."

The image dissolved from one of the rolling hills of Paradise Valley, to an area of farmland bordering Paradise Cove, to one of Niko perched casually on his desk. He wore a black suit with matching tie and a smile.

"Hello. I'm Niko Drake. And I approve this message."

Monique didn't even realize that she'd leaned forward until she had to sit back. *He's extremely photogenic. That ad for him works perfectly.* She had no doubt that more female votes were garnered every time it ran.

"That's what I need, a public service announcement."

Reaching for her phone, she quickly tapped the screen showing his number. As always, simply hearing his voice did things to her body and mind. "Hello, beautiful."

"Good morning, Niko."

"Whoa! Is it? You sound horrible."

"My campaign manager just said the same thing."

"Do you need for me to bring you anything? Orange juice maybe, or soup?"

"That's nice of you, but no, I'll be all right."

"What do you have over there for that cold, or flu, or whatever it is?"

"I took the last of my Alka-Seltzer Plus last night. I'll get some more when I go out later this afternoon."

"No, you won't. Give me an hour and I'll be over."

"You don't know my address."

"You're going to tell me."

"Niko, why do we keep having this conversation? This is a small town. You know how I feel about our being linked socially."

"I'll disguise myself as a deliveryman and be there in an hour."

Her laugh turned into a coughing fit.

"I won't take no for an answer."

Begrudingly, she gave her address. "But, Niko, wait."

He didn't. She called his name again and was answered by dead air.

"Just great," she moaned, dragging herself off the couch. With company coming over, the least she could do was jump in the shower and put on some clothes.

On second thought, given who was getting ready to darken her doorstep and donning attire…maybe not.

Chapter 17

Just a little over an hour later, her doorbell rang. She threw back the knitted afghan that covered her and padded over to the door. Her eyes narrowed as she looked out of her peephole. After another look, she opened the door.

"You're crazy," she said by way of greeting. She stepped aside to let him in.

"How'd I do?"

Niko stood in front of her wearing a tan workman's shirt, tan slacks, tennis shoes and a baseball cap. For him he was dressed down, but nothing could mask the tall, lean body and, now that he'd taken off his sunglasses, those sexy, dark eyes.

"I guess you could pass for a repairman if one didn't get too close." They stepped inside her living room. "How'd you get here? That fancy sports car that was parked in your garage?"

"No, a man on a worker's salary couldn't afford that. I borrowed one of my employee's vehicles."

"What does he drive?"

"A '94 Jeep."

Monique stood there shaking her head. She looked at the bag he held. "What's all in there?"

"Stuff to make you feel better." He walked into her kitchen as if he owned it, setting down the bag and pulling out its contents. "This is the best chicken noodle soup in town."

"Where'd you get it?"

"My mama's kitchen."

Monique stepped over and pulled off the lid. She was immediately assailed by the smell of spices, and steam wafting up from the still-warm broth. "Yum," she said as she sniffed. "Your mother made this?"

"Her chef did." He continued pulling out products. "Here we have orange juice, fresh lemons, honey, cayenne pepper—"

"Seriously?"

"Not familiar with home remedies, I see. We're about to change all that."

"With cayenne pepper? Don't bet on it."

"Then I probably shouldn't bet on this, either, huh?" He pulled out a small bottle of liquor along with a bottle of maple syrup.

"Now you've totally lost me."

"Never heard of a hot toddy?"

"Yes."

"Ever had one?"

"No."

"I'll make you one. It will help you feel better."

"Being as I'm not much of a drinker, I'll probably feel worse."

"You won't even taste the liquor. I promise you." He adopted a Southern accent. "It's good for what ails you."

"Ha! Don't even try it. Cowboy boots and your love of fishing aside, I don't think there's a country bone in your body."

"You'd be wrong." He pulled out the rest of what he'd brought over, including over-the-counter medical aids for cold and flu, then folded the paper bag and sat on the bar stool at the counter separating the kitchen and living space. "On summers, when we visited the grandparents in New Orleans, my grandfather would have us doing all sorts of things that would get us thrown out of the cool club with our friends back here. He made sure we could shoot, fish, ride horses…"

"And make hot toddies?"

"No, that comes courtesy of the family patriarch, Papa Dee."

"Another grandfather?"

"He's my great-grandfather. Still alive and happily kicking at one hundred and one."

"Wow! That's amazing."

"It really is. We had a scare on his one hundredth birthday. The Southern Cal cousins threw him a big party. We all were there along with about a hundred others. I think he got overly excited. Thankfully there was a doctor among us. He's fully recovered."

"Thank goodness."

"No doubt. That doctor, she—"

He was interrupted by Monique's rumbling stomach, evidence that she'd done nothing but drink tea all morning.

"Someone's hungry."

"Thanks to smelling that soup, I might finally have an appetite." She walked over to the cabinet and pulled down a bowl. "Want some?" she asked over her shoulder.

"No, I've already eaten, thank you. That's all yours."

"What about something to drink?"

"Orange juice sounds good."

While pouring his orange juice and then heating the soup, Monique couldn't help but think about Rob's recent visit and how much different it felt to have Niko here. There was no tension, at least none of the negative kind. Conversation flowed, and it felt, well, comfortable. As though his being in her home was the most natural thing in the world.

"Are you sure you don't want anything?" Monique asked, as she prepared to join him at the counter.

He looked at her pointedly. "Not right now."

Instead of responding, Monique set down the bowl before walking over to a box of tissues on a living-room table. She took one out, blew her nose and returned to the counter, immediately digging into the steaming bowl of soup. "This is delicious," she said after several spoonfuls.

"I'm glad you're enjoying it." He stood and looked around the room. "I like your place."

"Thank you."

"Hey, how's Devante, and what is he doing for work with the school burned down?"

"He went back to L.A."

"He can move around like that?"

"He wasn't supposed to. He got mad and left."

"Why?"

"They questioned him about the fire."

"According to Lawrence, they questioned several people."

"Not the same as him." She recounted what had happened. "I think someone genuinely believed he did it. I hate that he went back to the city. So many temptations. I hope he'll be all right."

She finished the bowl and turned it up to drain the broth. He smiled and walked over for his juice. She slid off the stool, placed the bowl in the sink, poured a glass of water and walked into the living room. He followed. She sat on the couch and pulled the afghan over her, feeling cold even though she was dressed in a sweatshirt and jeans. Niko sat on the love seat nearby.

"I saw your commercial," she said after once again blowing her nose. "It's good."

"Thank you."

"I know it's not kosher to share secrets with the enemy, but I was wondering who did it for you and how much it cost."

"Is that why you called me?"

"Yes, but I wasn't sure you'd want to provide that information."

"Sure I will. But I'm going to fix that hot toddy while I do." He fixed the tealike potion, then spent the next half hour talking about the media in general and producing commercials in particular, finishing up by giving her the name of his producer contact. "He's pretty cool," Niko finished, "and will probably work with you on pricing. Just tell him your budget and he'll come up with something within those boundaries."

"Thank you, Niko. This is very kind." She held up the near-empty mug. "And this is very good. It's spicy-hot, but my nose is clearing. I'm actually feeling a little better overall. Sleepy, though."

"My great-grandfather, Papa Dee, says that sleep is a healer." He stood. "So perhaps I should go and leave you to it."

Her eyes drooping, Monique prepared to rise.

"No, don't get up. I can let myself out. Lie there and get your rest." He walked over and positioned the afghan around her, taking the extra pillow that had been thrown on a nearby chair and propping it under her head. "There. All warm and cozy?"

"Yes," she said, sinking deeper into her plush couch and pulling up the afghan. Her eyes fluttered closed. "I think I'll just sleep…for…a little while."

Niko stared down at her for several long seconds. "You

do that," he finally whispered, bending to place a kiss on her brow. And then again, on her lips. And another.

She opened her eyes. "Thank you, Niko. You're a good man."

He left shortly after, making sure the door locked behind him. She drifted off into dreamland, believing that she could stand being tucked in by that man for, oh, say, the rest of her life.

Chapter 18

"Niko, it's Monique."

"Hey, Mo."

"It's funny hearing you call me that."

"That's what's on your campaign posters. Who'd ever vote for a mayor named Mo?"

"Probably the ones who preferred that to Nicodemus."

"Ouch! I was named after a great man."

"Perhaps, but you started it."

A week had passed since Niko had played doctor and brought healing potions, his presence included, into her house. They'd exchanged a few phone calls and texts, their camaraderie growing with each exchange.

"I just called to thank you for the information you gave me. I have a meeting with the producer later today. He's really creative and has already given me some great ideas. You were also right in that he is flexible and able to work within my budget. So, again, thanks so much."

"You're welcome. How are you feeling?"

"Much better."

"Good. You sound better."

"Yes, I had a very good doctor."

His voice dropped an octave. "Is that right."

"Yes." Her voice became sexy, flirty. "He's really good."

"Good. You can thank him tonight."

Monique swallowed, gripped her phone tighter as she asked, "How?"

"By buying me a hamburger."

"What?" Niko laughed. This was obviously not the answer she'd expected. "Are you serious?"

"Mo, I don't play when it comes to food. Do you have any appointments tonight?"

Monique checked her calendar. "Aside from the video-production meeting, no, I don't."

"Then what about seven-thirty, at the Cove Café?"

"You're determined to get gossip started, aren't you?"

"Why are you worried about wagging tongues?"

"Because perception is reality and I don't need any type of scandal smearing my name. You're in the lead and feel there's no need to worry. But I'm coming for you, Niko. I promise you that."

"What time is your appointment with the producer?"

"Five-thirty."

"Move it to seven and have him join us. That way it won't be just us two." When she remained quiet, he told her, "I want to see you, all right?"

"I'll see if he can change his schedule. If so, I'll see you then."

"Bring your big wallet. Since you're paying, I'm going to go for the triple-decker."

"For sharing your commercial producer with me? I'll even let you order fries."

Another busy day made the time pass quickly. Monique had asked the producer to meet her at six-thirty, so she'd have a half hour to talk over strategy before Niko arrived. Scott was a young, bright recent college graduate with a degree in film production. He worked at the public station to hone his chops with plans to move to a bigger commercial market next year. Most importantly, he was passionate about what he did and obviously very good at it. She told him her goals and overall vision. He presented ideas on how to best convey that in thirty seconds. By the time Niko joined them, just after seven, Monique felt confident about the plans that had been made.

"Well," Niko said following their greeting, "I see my opponent didn't want to show her hand."

"Nothing personal," Monique replied, a sly smile matching her devilishly twinkling eyes.

"Of course not!"

The three got down to the business of ordering, but just as the waitress came over, Scott's phone rang. He listened, a slight frown instantly marring his face. "Does she have a fever?" He gathered his things. "No, it's okay. I'll stop by the store and be home in a minute. Okay. Love you, too." He hung up and gave Monique and Niko an apologetic look. "Sorry, guys. I've got to run."

"Is everything all right?" Monique asked.

"I've got a little one who's teething. She's not too happy right now. I'd like to stay, but the wife needs some things from the store."

"No worries, man," Niko said, rising to shake Scott's hand. "Go take care of your daughter."

Once Scott left and Niko sat back down, he picked up his menu. "Sorry about that."

"It wasn't your fault." Monique perused the menu, as well.

"True, but I know how you hate to be seen alone with me."

She looked around. "It's pretty crowded and nice and bright in here. Plus, we're on opposite sides of the table. I think we make an innocent-enough-looking tableau."

"I concur."

The waitress came back over and took their orders.

"You weren't kidding about the triple burger," Monique said with a laugh. "A pound of ground sirloin? That would last me for days."

"I have a voracious appetite, what can I say?"

Thoughts of what she was hungry for could get her in trouble. Time to change the subject. "I finally had real conversations with Buddy and Dick."

"What's your impression?"

"They were a lot as you said they'd be. Dick was pleasantly patronizing. I don't think he very much likes the idea of my running against him. Buddy is passionate about his causes, which I admire. He'll be good for this town."

"I agree with everything you just said." He nodded at one person, waved at another. "There's a question I've been meaning to ask you."

"What's that?"

"The guy you were with the other night, Rob. I haven't seen him in town before. Who is he?"

"An ex who is still a good friend."

At least he'd been before they'd argued. She still hadn't heard from him, and the concert was next week. Lance might get his wish after all.

"I admire people who can remain friends after dating. That has rarely worked for me." The increasingly irate messages Ashley had left during the week because he'd refused her invites were solid proof.

"It's not easy. But Rob and I were friends before we began dating."

"They say being friends before lovers is the way to go. What happened, if you don't mind my asking?"

"Rob wanted to get married."

"And you didn't?"

After a long pause, Monique answered, "Not to him."

"But you do want to get married?"

"Someday." Monique looked at Niko, her expression unreadable. "When the right man comes along. What about you? Are you a confirmed, lifelong bachelor?"

"I'm not afraid of commitment. I love family, love children, and hope one day to have them."

"So what are you waiting on?"

Niko didn't hesitate in his answer. "The right woman."

Her comeback was interrupted by a familiar face approaching their table. The woman gave Monique a dismissive once-over. "Is this why you haven't returned my calls?"

Niko looked up. "Hello, Ashley."

Providing Monique a clear view of her back, Ashley focused on Niko. "Is this why you've been running from me and are no longer available for conversation or to share a drink?"

"Does it look like I'm running from you now?"

"You know you've been avoiding me. Don't even try to lie."

Other than a brief tightening of his jaw, Niko showed no outer signs of irritation. "You have my attention now, Ashley. What do you want?"

"If you'd returned one of several messages left on your phone, you'd already know. I want to play a more active and pivotal role in your campaign."

"And I texted back the contact number for volunteers, though allowing me to place promotional items in your salon has been very helpful."

Ashley changed tactics: lowered her voice, smiled seductively and lazily ran a hand up Niko's arm. "I'd like a more…personal role, you know, work with you directly to ensure the win. Unless you've found another way to shut down your competition, put some of that good Niko lov—"

"That's enough." His voice was low yet deadly. "Don't cause a scene."

Ashley bit back a retort and sat down, uninvited, at their table. Still she ignored Monique.

"Is this any way to treat a friend?"

Niko took a patient breath. "I apologize for not returning your calls. Between the campaign and company business, it's been a jam-packed week."

"Apology accepted." She leaned toward him, close enough for her tank-top-covered breast to graze his arm. "But only if after you leave here, you'll stop by my place for drinks."

He moved his arm away from her chest. "That won't be possible."

"Why not?"

He looked at Monique, who was tactfully viewing the exchange. "Forgive my rudeness."

A not-so-subtle jab at this intruder's impolite behavior. "Ashley, have you met Mo Slater? She is an accomplished attorney who is running on the Democratic ticket. Mo, this is Ashley DeWitt."

"Niko, can we talk privately for a moment?" For the attention Ashley gave her, Monique might as well have been invisible.

"I'm afraid not. Monique and I are having dinner and discussing the mayoral race. Whatever else you need to say to me can be shared here."

"Trust me," Ashley purred with a flip of her long brown hair and a smile. "What I have to say is for your ears alone."

"If it's that private, I'm not interested."

"Fine!" She gave Monique a cold look and stood. "I'll take my information elsewhere."

"Goodbye, Ashley."

She turned abruptly, almost knocking over the waitress delivering Niko's triple-decker and Monique's chicken cordon bleu sandwich.

"Sorry about that," Niko said once Ashley and the waiter had left. "Jealousy, possessiveness and constant drama are some of the reasons we broke up. I thought we had an understanding, but she's falling back into old ways. You can't imagine…"

Monique offered a sympathetic smile as she spread her napkin. "Unfortunately, Niko, I can."

Chapter 19

The Silver Serenade Concert was finally here. Dapper men and gorgeous, gown-clad women filled The Regency Center and shone brighter than the lights that dangled across the Golden Gate Bridge. A buzz of excitement was in the air as some of the one thousand lucky patrons who'd secured this hot ticket sipped wine, champagne and spirits, while others threw air-kisses to just-seen friends. Monique stepped into the lobby, accompanied by her campaign manager, Lance.

"Oh, my God," he quietly squealed as he looked around. "This is fabulous! I should probably be sorry that Rob couldn't come." Pregnant pause. "But I'm not!"

Monique didn't mind that Rob wasn't there, either. But she was glad that he'd finally sent her an email stating he was okay and would call her soon.

"You fit right in," she said, brushing a stray piece of lint from Lance's lapel. And he did. Handsome enough to be a model, Lance wore a black Giorgio Armani tux with pale-pink-and-silver-striped shirt and silver bow tie. His raven-black hair was slicked back in a debonair fashion, bringing out the angular lines of his face and the stark blueness of his eyes.

Said blue eyes were shining. "I'm going to look like a groupie but I've got to take pictures. Brandon will be so jealous. He would have loved this!" He pulled out his phone and snapped a surprised Monique, underscoring his point.

"Monique, darling!" It was Margo. Monique turned, immediately aware that her godmother was in her element with diamonds dripping, silver silk swirling and not one hair out of place.

She reached where Monique and Lance were standing and held out her arms, first hugging Lance and then Monique. "You look positively radiant!" Margo stepped back to look at her goddaughter. "I love it when you wear your hair down. And I told you that the dress I ordered was perfect. You look positively stunning!"

"Thank you, Margo. I never would have chosen silver as a gown color, but I must say, this darker shade is beautiful."

When Margo had told Monique that silver attire was strongly recommended for the Silver Serenade Concert, Monique had balked. "Silver? No, Margo, that will wash out my skin. I'll look ashy, like I went to the mall for lotion and they were sold out!"

"I'd seen that gown earlier in a fashion magazine and had immediately thought of you. It's a darker shade of silver, and I knew it would complement your tone perfectly. The earrings, necklace—" she looked down "—your shoes. You should really tip your stylist. She did you a grand."

"She put me together," Monique said to Lance. "Thank you, Margo, for doing an amazing job. And you, lady." She shook her head as Margo let the silver fox boa slip from her shoulders. "I'm sure you must know that you're the belle of the ball."

"The competition was fierce for which one of us would shine the brightest." Margo looked around, her sixty-plus-year-old eyes shining. "I think my sparkle is pretty bright, if I must say so myself. Oh, I see some of those ladies now. Come, let's go over so I can introduce you to the board."

Lance chose to stay and people watch while Monique and Margo crossed the lobby and entered a room for VIPs. There were uniformed waiters offering various hors d'oeuvres and flutes of champagne. In here, the air was rarefied. The bougie of the bougie, Monique thought, as she imagined that the jewels alone worn by the women could probably fund a third-world country for about ten years. After Margo introduced her to the board, they continued around the room, greeting Margo's other friends. Surreptitiously, she scanned the crowd, looking for Niko without consciously realizing it. They hadn't talked since sharing the meal at Cove Café. Crazy, but she missed him and was almost certain he'd attend.

They made the rounds. She didn't see him or any of the Drakes, for that matter. Surprise and disappointment vied for dominance, even as she spotted several Paradise Cove citizens. Thankful for the diversion, she began chatting them up. Margo left abruptly, before Monique could ask about the whereabouts of the Drakes. Figuring she'd find out soon enough, Monique continued talking with a man who owned several Paradise Cove businesses. She had just accepted a flute of champagne when an undeniable murmur spread across the room. About the same time her heart twisted. And somehow, innately, she knew. He was here. At the mere thought of seeing him again, she smiled and slowly turned around.

And there he was—handsome, even dastardly—parting a path in the room with his aura much like Moses did the Red Sea. The smile froze on her face and she was thankful for it. Because it gave the false impression that she was okay with the fact that he was not alone.

"Wow," the Paradise Cove resident she'd been talking to commented. "Your opponent surely knows how to make an entrance. Niko has gone and brought Cinderella to the ball."

Monique didn't respond, couldn't. But had she answered, she would have had to agree. Niko's date was tall, equaling Niko's height in her red-bottomed heels. She wore a wine-colored gown, which highlighted her tanned skin and jet-black hair, and stood out in a sea of silver. Even from across the room, Monique could tell that her features were flawless, her smile was radiant and she was exactly the type of woman Niko would choose. They made a perfect pair.

She wanted to head to the ladies' room a moment to clear her head. But it wasn't meant to be. Monique was cornered by a prominent citizen whose grandchildren attended Paradise Cove Elementary. She didn't stop to take a breath while making a very strong case to have a full-scale fire department built in the town within the next two years. Monique listened, while taking small steps toward the hall that led to the ladies' room.

"It should come before a hospital," the woman added. "If we'd had one, the school may have been saved. And we've got a top-notch medical facility just thirty minutes away!"

After listening for as long as she could without appearing rude, she reached for the woman's hand. "You've made an excellent point. If elected, my team will take everything you've said under careful advisement. Please excuse me. There's something I need to do."

That thing she'd told Niko she never did. Run!

But it was too late. When she looked up, there he was.

"Hello, Gladys," he said to the woman who'd barred Monique's escape. He turned to her with hand outstretched. "Good evening, Monique."

"Good evening, Niko."

"You look lovely."

"Thank you."

"Monique, I'd like you to meet Zaria Hakimi. Zaria, this is Monique Slater, my formidable mayoral opponent."

Zaria smiled at Monique sincerely. "It is a pleasure to meet you," she said, with hand outstretched.

She was even more beautiful up close, Monique decided as she worked to get five measly letters past her suddenly dry lips. She was flustered, angry at herself for how she was feeling, and chose to try to regain her footing by putting her relationship to him in perspective.

"Hello." She shook Zaria's hand. "Are you a resident of Paradise Cove?"

"Not yet," she said, looking directly at Monique, though the comment was clearly not meant for her.

"It's a wonderful place to live. And should you decide to move there…I'd like to be your mayor."

Zaria chuckled, a wonderful sound, like bells in the breeze. Her lyrical accent was equally charming. She turned to Niko. "Going after your supporters right in your face. I like her." Her eyes swept Monique's attire. "I love what you're wearing. That color is perfect for you."

Seriously? Did she have to be beautiful and a nice person, too? "It doesn't compare to your gown," Monique responded. "It's just amazing. With all of the crystals and that lace? I could never wear something like that, but on you, it's effortless."

She looked down just as Niko slid his arm around Zaria's waist. It was more a gentlemanly than possessive gesture, but a monster greener than the emerald ring on Zaria's finger sidled up beside her and whispered, *Wish it were you?*

She was saved from her own thoughts when Niko's parents walked up.

"Monique, have you met my mother?" Niko asked.

"No, I haven't had the pleasure."

Monique greeted Ike Sr. and met Jennifer, who along with some of their children had been backstage talking to some of the organizers of tonight's gala. She also said hello to Ike Jr. and his date before finally escaping when Lance found her and pulled her away.

"Enjoy the evening," she said to the general group in parting. Niko looked at Monique. Outwardly his expression was casual, but Monique had studied his eyes enough to know that there was something going on in that well-groomed, close-cropped head of his.

Two hours later, after the last encore, she found out exactly what it was.

Chapter 20

"Monique!"

She'd almost made it, had navigated the room and the lobby and the crowd so that she could leave the event without running into him, without having to smile at him and Zaria again. If she hurried, she thought, she could reach the door and make her exit without turning around. Later she'd swear that she didn't hear him call her name. On a stack of Bibles. In a packed courtroom with the honorable judge whomever presiding. *Five more feet—ten, max—and I'll be free.*

Except for the iron-grip hold on her elbow, just before she reached the door; close enough to feel the wind blowing from outside. There was no escaping. So she turned around. "Yes, Niko?"

"Come with me."

As if she had a choice. He'd lessened his hold but hadn't let go of her arm. Now he led them down a short hallway, away from the crowd.

Finally, away from prying eyes, she jerked away. "What do you want?"

"I know you're running. And I know why. The Hakimis are longtime family friends. We've known each other for years. Zaria and I have known each other since we were teenagers."

"Good for you."

"There is not now nor has there ever been anything romantic between us. I've never felt for her what I feel for you. I'm tired of us trying to deny what's unavoidable, trying to be politically correct and do the right thing because we're in a race against each other." His phone buzzed. "Look, let's get away from town gossip and prying eyes. Meet me in half an hour."

"I'm not going to a hotel with you, Niko. There's too many people from P.C. here. I won't—"

"Shh. Listen. We don't have much time." He pulled out a card. "My driver, the same one who took you home the other night, is right outside. He's waiting to take you to my condo."

"I don't think so."

"Please, Monique. Trust me on this. We need to discuss this situation. And we need to talk tonight."

Before she could argue, he kissed her and was gone.

Within minutes, she was in the back of a town car, riding through the streets of San Francisco, texting instructions to Lance, leaving a message for Margo and believing that from one single kiss she'd surely lost her mind!

They entered an exclusive neighborhood with beautiful homes and winding roads. The car stopped at the very top, in front of a stately building. The lawn was intricately landscaped and lights cast a soft glow all around.

The driver got out of the car and opened her door. "Here's the key, Ms. Slater," he said once he'd helped her exit. "His door is the one on the right. Go right on in. Niko will be here momentarily." He watched until she'd opened the door and waved. Then he was gone.

To call what she viewed a condo felt like a misnomer. With high, vaulted ceilings, chandeliers and a winding staircase, this place felt like a castle. She pulled off her shoes and had barely begun a self-guided tour when she heard the door open.

"Monique?"

Her heart began beating wildly before she could respond, as if her body knew something that she didn't. She walked from the dining room to the living room, where he stood.

"Your place is beautiful," she said when she reached him.

"And so are you."

With no further words, he pulled her into his arms, their lips immediately connecting in a torrid kiss. Hands were everywhere—chest, breasts, hips, thighs, back, neck and buttocks.

"I know I said we'd talk, but right now there's something else I'd much rather do." His eyes were clear and pleading. "Do you want me, too?"

"Yes." She was breathless and so incredibly hot. Later, it would be the only reason she could think of for her next line. "Unzip me," she said and turned around.

He did, kissing each inch of skin as it became exposed. She wore no bra and now, standing before him with only a silky white thong and stilettos, felt suddenly shy.

"Don't." He placed a finger under her chin and lifted her head. "There is no reason to hide perfection. You are beautiful." He took off his jacket and placed it around her shoulders. "I'm so ready to make love to you, but I don't want to rush this moment." He walked over and opened a console hidden in a panel on the wall. Soon the sounds of soft R & B surrounded them. He took off his bow tie and unbuttoned the top buttons on his tuxedo shirt. "Let me get us something to take upstairs."

Moments later he came out of the kitchen with a wine bucket and two glasses. In the meantime, Monique had picked up her gown and now carried it over her arm. She was still wearing Niko's jacket. And the heels.

"Wait here." Niko walked up the stairs and disappeared. When he returned, his hands were empty. Without a word he walked over and picked up Monique.

"What are you doing?" she said with a gasp, having been taken totally by surprise.

"Isn't it obvious?" He began walking up the stairs as though she were as light as a feather. "I'm sweeping you off your feet."

They reached the master suite, which offered an unobstructed view of the heart of San Francisco. Lights twinkled from afar, rivaling the stars for brightness. Low flames burned in the fireplace. The music surrounded them. It was like a fairy tale.

"You lit candles?" Monique exclaimed softly when he returned with the wine. "And the fire." Her voice was hushed.

"I like how it sets the mood." He walked to her and put his arms around her. "Ms. Slater, are you in the mood?"

The song changed. Strands of the prelude to a slow jam by Bruno Mars filled the room. Its melody was sweet, and sexy, like the moment. Niko began to rock back and forth, dancing with Monique in his arms. She placed her arms around his neck.

"What in the world am I doing here?"

"What you've been wanting to do for a long time. What we've both wanted." They kissed again. Niko's hand eased inside the tuxedo jacket and across her skin. Monique, normally not known as the aggressor, deepened the kiss and pressed her body against him. He moaned. She nipped his neck.

Playtime was over.

Niko guided her to sit on the edge of the bed. Looking

into her eyes, he slowly removed one sandal, and then the other, all the while putting whispery kisses on her ankle, calf, knee, thigh...

Monique gasped and lay back.

"That's right," he whispered, his breath hot on her inner thigh, his mustache tickling her sensitive skin. "Relax and enjoy." With infinite patience, he ran a finger along the rim of her thong, pulling the flimsy material aside. He kissed her in the most intimate of ways, his tongue running between her already wet folds, over and again. She spread her legs. He took her unspoken suggestion to go deeper: licking, nipping, driving her wild. Soon a strong, long forefinger joined in the dance. He sucked her pebbled pearl into his mouth, while stroking to give her pleasure. Before Monique knew it, she was shaking, screaming, as an orgasm more intense than she'd ever felt erupted.

"Niko!"

"Yes?" He stood, removed his clothes.

"That...was...amazing."

She hadn't seen amazing until she opened her eyes and looked at him. She raised up to better admire the view. There, in the shadow of the fire, he looked like a sculpted god: arms, chest and legs toned and muscled. Not too much, but just right. What captivated Monique most of all was the muscle between his legs, hard and thick, ready for action. She wasn't a virgin, but Monique knew she'd never experienced someone like him in her life. After reaching into his pants pocket for a condom, he lay on the bed.

"Come here."

She complied. The dance began again, his kisses, all over her face. Leisurely, thoroughly, they tasted each other, exploring what both had so long admired, languishing in the knowledge that they were safely away from prying eyes. Here, they weren't Niko Drake and Monique Slater the mayoral candidates. Here they were two people making sweet love.

He lowered his head and kissed her neck and shoulders, running his finger over one breast and the next. Lower still, and he pulled a nipple into his mouth. Monique tried to reciprocate and kiss him where she could.

"Relax and enjoy," he said again. And she did.

After running his tongue all over her body, he covered her, running a finger along her nether lips. "Mmm, you're so wet and ready for me."

"Yes." Boldly, she reached for his weighty shaft, ran her finger around its mushroom tip. His eyes bored into hers as she stroked him. Long. Thick. Amazing.

He entered her, oh, so slowly, filling her fuller than she ever had been. He'd pull out a bit and push in deeper, over and again, until they were truly one. After several seconds, her body relaxed and adjusted to his girth. He moaned, shifted his hips and began a familiar thrusting as old as time. Monique matched his rhythm, lifting herself to meet his plunging heat.

"You feel so good," he whispered, raising her leg to subtly shift their position. "So…good." Reaching beneath them, he squeezed her booty, grabbed her hips and led the dance. He alternated the experience—fast, slow, thrust, grind—creating a friction so delicious that tears came to her eyes. And once again, from deep in her core the quaking started, unfurling through her body and her soul until she cried out in relief. Niko followed suit, his explosion handled in silence as he squeezed Monique tightly against him.

Slowly, he released her and placed a kiss on her temple. "That was incredible."

She turned, traced the line of his jaw while gazing into his eyes. "All I can say is wow."

"Spend the night with me?"

She nodded.

So without saying a word, without making a sound, the two lovers cuddled into each other's arms, Niko pulled a cover over them…and they fell into a satiated, peaceful sleep.

Chapter 21

Monique snuggled deeper into the covers, repositioning her pillow for a more comfortable fit. She turned her head, and when she did, a sliver of light beamed on her eye. She scrunched up her face. The shades in her bedroom were specially designed to keep out light. So how was it coming through? She opened one eye, and then the other. Lifting her head, she looked around, disoriented at first, and then as she noted the now empty bottle of wine, the two used glasses and now burned-down candles, the night before came rushing back. She flopped onto her back. When shifting her legs, she felt a delicious ache that left no doubt as to whether she'd been dreaming. She had spent the night with Niko and made what felt like endless love.

Niko. Where was he? In answer, she heard humming and footsteps coming up the stairs. Just before he entered, so did the smell of coffee.

"Seriously, Niko? Breakfast in bed?"

She rolled over, sat up and used the sheet to cover herself.

Niko walked to her side of the bed, placed the tray across her lap and kissed her forehead. "Good morning."

"Good morning. My goodness, look at this. How long have you been up?"

"Not long. This isn't much—eggs, muffins, fresh-squeezed juice."

"It's perfect." Monique dug into the fluffy scrambled eggs, aware that she'd not really eaten last night and was now starving. "What about you?"

"I've already eaten."

"I could get used to this."

"Is that so?"

After a couple more bites, Monique wiped her mouth with a napkin. "We probably should talk about what's happened."

"You weren't trying to talk last night. Or two hours later when I woke you up."

"If you'll remember, I was busy doing other things with my mouth."

"You surprised me."

"Oh, really?"

"In public, you're always so serious, no-nonsense, re-served. But here—" he ran a finger along her thigh "—I got to experience that fire that sometimes flashes in your eyes, the passion that's helped make you successful. I really like you, Monique, and have felt this way long before we had sex."

"Yes, there was no doubt about the attraction."

"You know what this means?"

"What?"

"There's no going back to how we were. I want more of this, more of us."

"This is crazy! We're running against each other. How is this supposed to work?"

"We can start by leaving politics out of our bed. Out there, we're opponents. But when we're alone—" he kissed her nose, cheek, mouth "—we're on the same side. As for spending time together, we'll find a way. Okay?"

"We'll see."

Sunday night, they both returned to Paradise Cove. For Monique, the woman who returned to the condo was very different from the one who'd left. *Enthralled* was how she felt about Niko. She refused to call it love.

"Mo, are you ready?"

Lance and two assistants from the campaign office had joined Monique in downtown P.C. They were taping a segment for her campaign advertisement. Excitement mixed with nerves. In the two weeks since the Silver Serenade Concert, footage of Monique on the campaign trail—visiting the elderly, accessing the fire-damaged school, talking with farmers, even trying to milk a cow—had been gathered. A camera crew of two had followed her the entire time, getting action footage to use in the commercial. Her on-screen delivery was the only thing left to film. This was happening today.

Because of the attention she'd had to pay to her cases, including a two-day trip to Los Angeles, she'd seen Niko only in passing. But they'd talked by phone. He wanted to see her. She reminded him what was at stake if they found themselves the focus of small-town talk. "What if a rumor knocks both of us out and Dick gets in?" she'd asked him after one night when she'd almost given in to desire. "Then P.C. would really be in trouble." Niko had backed off for a couple of days, but his scorching late-night phone calls had once again reminded her of what was only ten minutes away.

A small group huddled on a sidewalk downtown, across the street from a bank that anchored one corner and a bakery the next. The town's governmental buildings—city hall, post office and the like—were on the opposite side of the street, where the final shots would take place. But first they'd shoot the tagline, with Monique walking down the main downtown street. It was a small crew, just a camera-

man, a production assistant, a stylist and Scott, the director. But it was a rather slow Tuesday morning with nothing
going on, so the shoot attracted attention.

After making sure the sidewalk was clear and the shot
was set, Scott walked to Monique. "Okay, just walk naturally from that mark over to here. Stand, hold and talk
naturally, the way we practiced, just like you're talking
to me. Are you ready?"

Monique nodded. She tried not to look at the early-
morning shoppers and curious onlookers stopping to see
what was going on. Instead, she ran the lines over in her
mind. After the makeup artist patted the shine and Scott
counted her down, Monique took a breath and, while casually walking, delivered her lines.

At least that was the plan.

But just as she began walking, a movement caught
the side of her eye. Niko. He'd obviously parked while
she'd been distracted and leaned, arms crossed, against
his sports car. Black shirt and sunglasses. Tall, tanned
and confident. Looking as though he'd just stepped from
a fashion magazine. Reminding her of why most nights
she'd tossed and turned, unable to sleep. Because her body
craved him.

"Cut!" Scott walked over to her. "It's okay, Monique.
This is your first time on camera. It's harder than it looks.
Just go back to your mark and start again."

She did. Twice. The angrier she got with herself for not
being able to focus and concentrate on the few words she
had to deliver, the more she messed them up, and not because she'd never done this before. She was just about to
walk over and tell Niko to please stop staring and move
on. But when she looked up, he was gone. So with renewed
determination, and a sigh of relief, she walked briskly to
her mark, waited until Scott signaled that tape was roll-

ing and said, "I'm Monique Slater with a new vision for a new day. Together we can make Paradise Cove truly heaven on earth."

Less than an hour later, they took a break. Lance walked over to where they were viewing the footage on a digital camera. He handed her a bottle of water. "You did great."

"After getting over a case of nerves, I did all right."

"This looks good," Scott said to Monique. "Let's wrap it up, guys."

"Thank you, Scott." They hugged. "You're right. This is harder than it looks."

"Now you know why Hollywood gets paid the big bucks."

"Can you shoot me a copy of the finished product before it airs?"

"Absolutely. We should have it put together in the next day or so. I'll give you a call."

Monique returned to the office. Forgetting that she'd turned off her phone during the shoot, she was surprised to see a couple of missed calls and several text messages. She read the texts first. All from Niko:

Hello, beautiful.

Am I bothering you?

Damn! If I weren't running, I'd vote for you myself!

In spite of her maddening frustration with this man, she smiled as she remembered that on her last glance over before he left, he'd been holding his phone. She shook her head, swiping the phone screen so that she could hear the voice messages. To her surprise there were more than a dozen.

Several were work related, regarding either the L.A. office or various cases. One was from her mother. Three were from the campaign office. One was her insurance company. Two were telemarketing. One was from Niko... and one was from Rob.

She saved, deleted and skipped until she got to Niko's message, which was next to last. "Hello, movie star. Give me a call."

Laughing, she started to redial him right away but decided to listen to the last message:

"Hey, Mo. I finally got over being upset with you and wanted to call. You're undoubtedly busy, but buzz me when you can. I want to hear all about the concert."

Monique exhaled, relieved that Rob was no longer angry and that he wasn't making a case for winning her back. This message sounded normal. Finally, she hoped, he'd accepted what was.

She scrolled her contact list and dialed Niko. "Hey."

"Hello."

"I see you've got time to run around town and spy on your opponents. You must not have enough to do."

"My campaign office is downtown, Ms. Slater. Stopping by the bakery was a last-minute decision."

"You weren't at the bakery when I saw you. You were watching me in action, trying to get tips."

"Yes, I was enjoying the performance. But I left because I was making you nervous. Don't try to deny it."

"I wasn't going to."

Monique looked at her caller ID as another call came in. "Look, it's the office calling. I've got to run."

"Are you all right? You sound stressed."

"A little bit."

"I can help with that."

"I'd love that, actually. But the thought that someone would find out about it stresses me more."

"But otherwise you'd see me?"

"Of course. I'll talk to you later."

It was after nine o'clock when Monique finally returned home. The day had been productive but exhausting, a constant balancing act between the upcoming election and her casework. Lance was trying to recruit more volunteers for these last few months of campaigning. She'd be glad when it was over. All work and no play was taking its toll.

After fixing a sandwich, she called Rob. "I hope you don't mind my eating while we talk," she began after saying hello. "I just got home."

"I worry about how hard you work."

"This pace won't last forever."

"How are your chances looking to win this thing?"

"My numbers are climbing, but there's still a long way to go. Since I'm not from here, I not only have to sell my platform but myself, as well. People vote for who they feel they know. So I've had to put in overtime. How are you?"

"Keeping busy. I went to a couple Dodgers games."

"Sounds like fun."

"How was the concert?"

They talked comfortably for almost half an hour. She told him about the Silver Serenade. He caught her up on the goings-on of mutual friends. Once again, it felt like old times. Monique hoped their interactions would stay this way.

At ten o'clock, she crawled into bed. The usual tossing and turning ensued, so she lay there mapping out the next day's activities in her head. Suddenly, a thud sounded against the back of her house. She listened, lifted her head off the pillow and held her breath. There it was again. Her phone rang, startling her further.

"Hello?" A mumbling sound was all she heard. "Niko?"

Then, just above a whisper, "Back door. Let me in."

No way. Not even bothering to throw a robe over her thigh-high T-shirt, she marched downstairs. If this man had come over to her house unannounced…

Reaching the patio door, she snatched it open. Niko, dressed in black from head to toe, hurried inside, closing the blinds behind her.

"What in the—"

The rest of her question was swallowed in a kiss.

"Don't say a word," he ordered, after thoroughly tasting her. "Not until I'm finished."

He took her hand and headed for the stairs. She was too shocked to do anything but follow. They reached her bedroom.

He nodded toward her T-shirt. "Take that off."

Something about the way he said it, brooking no argument, was a total turn-on. Most of the time she was the one giving orders. Right now, following them felt like a wise idea. She pulled the oversize cotton top over her head.

"Lie down." He reached into a pouch strapped around his waist. "On your stomach."

She heard what sounded like paper rattling and a jar opening. The bed dipped from the weight of Niko getting on it. She felt him straddle her. Anticipation of the unknown was so intense that goose pimples broke out on her skin. Soon, something cool and soothing was being spread on her body. The smell of chocolate mixed with spices tickled her nose.

"Just relax," he whispered, methodically kneading her neck and shoulder blades until he felt them loosen up. Only then did he continue down her back, across her buttocks—which he gave considerable attention—and hips, down her thighs, shins and toes.

And everywhere his fingers landed…his lips followed. Who knew that between the toes was an erogenous zone?

"Turn over."

"I can barely move," she mumbled.

"Shh. Don't open your eyes."

This time, he started from the bottom. His fingers and tongue meandered from her ankle to her knee. A kiss here. A nibble there. He reached the insides of her thighs and spread her legs apart. His kisses teased her tender skin and brushed her heat.

And drove her mad.

He slid a finger between her folds, rubbed something cool and creamy on her jewel.

"Ooh." *That's cold.*

But not for long. His warm, strong tongue began licking the cream, slowly, deeply, and warmed her right up. He lapped first the edible massage oil and then her own sweet nectar like a thirsty man, buried his head between her legs and nibbled, sucked, flicked and massaged her spot until she was mewling with pleasure.

"Niko, please…"

After the sound of ripping foil, she felt the tip of his massive head against her heat, rubbing against her. She lifted her body in invitation and was rewarded by the feel of his mushroom tip entering her garden of love. He eased himself inside her, making her aware of every delicious inch.

"Oh, my God."

He pulled out just as slowly. Thrust. Pull. Plunge. Swerve. Finding first one nipple and then the other, sucking them into his mouth, swirling his tongue along with his hips, slamming into the depths of Monique's entire being, filling her up.

Over and again. Slow and then faster. Then more, until both were bathed in a thin sheen of sweat.

Then from behind.

Then Monique on top.

Then the pleasure of her mouth on him, taking him in—licking, stroking, sucking, squeezing—feeling him squirm and moan in satisfaction.

A final time he mounted her, determined to make her peak once more. Wanting to leave her so satiated that she could not move.

"Give it to me," he whispered, quickening the pace as she moaned and squealed. "I want all of this. I want all of you." He palmed her cheeks, going deeper, bonding them closer, until Monique's body shook with the force of her climax.

She fell back on the bed, totally whipped.

He rolled off and gently placed the cover over her nude body.

"I think I've relieved your stress," he whispered against her ear. "Now I can sleep peacefully. Good night, love."

When she awoke the next morning, Niko's visit felt like a dream. But her body, and the lingering scent of love and chocolate, told her otherwise.

After a long shower she felt ready to begin her day: happy, energized and stress-free.

Chapter 22

For the next three months, Niko and Monique settled into a workable if somewhat unorthodox arrangement. In Paradise Cove, they went about their separate business. Having crisscrossed the town of just under four thousand residents many times over, and with campaign ads running on not only community but also local stations, Monique turned her attention to the cases in which she was involved. Niko focused on handling the legal affairs for Drake Realty Plus, along with other corporate clients. As mind-blowing as the night had been when he'd come over, at her request it hadn't happened again. So on those occasions when both of their schedules were free, they returned to the condo in San Francisco for cozy dinners, stimulating conversations and uninterrupted lovemaking. It was as exasperating as it was exhilarating. The more Monique had, the more she wanted. When it came to private time together, there was never enough.

The same couldn't be said for public encounters. In a town this size, it was inevitable. Especially this Labor Day weekend, when the town held an annual event called Days of Paradise. Lance said that it was by far the biggest event of the year: parades, a fairground and a formal ball. Monique knew that she and Niko would be in the spotlight. And undoubtedly under the microscope. She'd have to be extra careful not to let her feelings for him show.

On her way to the parade, she rang her mother, prepared for the chiding that came with each call.

"About time we heard from you," her mother scolded, though Monique swore she could feel happiness seeping from the speakers. "You're going to run yourself ragged."

"I have been busy. But it's slowing down somewhat. I've been able to devote more time to my clients. And guess what. Today, I'm going to be in a parade!" She shared what she knew about the annual event that celebrated the town's incorporation. "People from neighboring towns attend, as well. There's not much ongoing entertainment, so this is a big deal."

"You sound happy, dear."

"I am. I balked at first, but now I'm looking forward to it. I'll be riding in a white convertible, wearing a white suit. I stopped at the cowboy hat that Lance suggested."

"How old is Lance?"

"Lance is married, Mom."

"Oh. I just hate to think of you in that town all alone."

"Margo's here. And the people are friendly." *And I'm in love with the man I'm running against.* No, that sounded crazy in thought, let alone voiced out loud.

"How is Emma? Has she had the baby yet?"

"She's not due for a few months. I need to give her a call."

"When you talk to her, tell her I said hello. What about Rob? Have you talked to him lately?"

"Yes, and he's doing well. The business is growing and it's baseball season. He's enjoying two of his favorite things."

"Your dad's here, Monique. Do you want to talk to him?"

Monique neared the park where the parade would begin. It appeared that all of P.C. had already arrived. "I'd love to, but I've arrived at the parade route and need to call Lance. It looks as though I'm one of the last to arrive. Give Dad my love. I'll call him tomorrow."

Lance found her before she could dial his number. They weaved through the throng of people to a side street where four brand-new convertibles gleamed in the morning sunshine. They were identical except for the colors: red, white, blue and black. The other candidates were already there. Niko, dressed casually in a black button-down and jeans, spoke as she passed.

"Don't forget to wave," he joked. "But remember to hold on."

She greeted the other candidates and met the driver for her car. Soon, they were on their way, heading down Main Street. Monique smiled, waved and tossed candy to the children lining the street. It was amazing to her how many faces she recognized and people she knew, when a few short months ago, they were strangers. After years in Los Angeles, she'd thought she'd go stir-crazy in a place this small. But the slow pace and simple life were growing on her. She'd run for mayor because it was what her godfather had wanted. She'd win because this little town was beginning to feel like home.

Niko was distracted, but he went through the motions: smiling, waving, calling out friends. He'd rarely missed this celebration and had been in the parade more times than he could remember. But this time was different. All his life he'd lived in this town. Soon, he'd be running it.

His car was right behind Monique's. A beautiful sight. She was excited, and it showed. Her smile was contagious and people were drawn to her warmth. She tossed her hair, exposed that part of her neck that he loved to nibble, turned to the side and the outline of her breast gave him pause. He shifted his gaze and his thoughts. He turned and looked again. Was that…? *No, couldn't have been. She would have told me.* The band reached their spot and began to play, and the thought was forgotten. It wouldn't come up again for the rest of the busy day.

In the wee hours of the morning, he called her. "Are you up?"

"Yes."

"You looked beautiful tonight."

"Thank you."

"Do you know how hard it was for me to watch other men dance with you, hold you and flirt as they looked into your eyes?"

"Yes, as a matter of fact I do, because of all of the ladies you spun around the room."

"It comes with the job, love."

"I know."

"It looks like you enjoyed yourself."

"I did, immensely. The parade was fun, the picnic was nice and tonight's ball was absolutely beautiful. I might pass on tomorrow's activities, though. This festival wears you out."

"Hey, when it's the only excitement in the year, you go full on."

"I see."

"The people love you. I saw how they interacted with you on the route. Here I'm thinking I'd outshine everybody, the old pro and all. But you're a natural."

"I believe I'm hitting my stride. Next month's debate is the last major public event before the election. Are you ready?"

"Of course."

"Buddy's a straight talker, but Dick… I'm going to have to watch him."

"I wouldn't worry about him. When shooting the breeze, he can talk your ear off. But he isn't as prolific in controlled settings."

"I think he'll hold his own."

"Babe, the craziest thing happened today. I'd forgotten about it until now."

"What?"

"During the parade, while looking and waving and everything, I could have sworn I saw that guy you dated."

"Rob?"

"Yes."

"No way."

"Yeah, that's what I said. Next time you talk to him, tell him he has a twin."

"They say we all do."

"You know I want to come over."

"I know. I want it, too. But I'm too paranoid. My neighbors are nosy."

"Then come over here."

"Maybe we can go to the condo next week."

Niko groaned. "Man, I'll be glad when this election is over and we can go public."

"You'll be satisfied being the mayor's man?"

"Ha! No, baby. It's you the mayor will satisfy."

"On that note, good night, Niko."

Her sarcastically delivered comment brought out the throaty chuckle she loved. "Good night."

Chapter 23

The residents of Paradise Cove filed into the crowded auditorium at city hall. It looked as though all three-thousand-plus residents had come to hear the candidates make their case for becoming their next mayor. There was a buzz of excitement in the air, not surprising considering that this was the first mayoral election in over a decade and the only time these candidates would debate.

Monique, Niko and the other two mayoral candidates, Republican Dick Schneider and Libertarian Buddy Gao, exchanged small talk while waiting inside a backstage room. Their assistants and a few city officials were also milling around. Niko was keenly aware of how good Monique looked, all conservative and professional in a navy suit, low-heeled navy pumps and pearls, while remembering how wild and receptive she was the other night when he'd pinned her against the shower wall with his powerful penis. Knowing the embarrassing situation that might occur from his line of thinking, and the desire that would only increase if he neared her, he turned to Dick, standing just a few feet away.

"I'm looking forward to debating you, Dick. This way we can clear up some of the rumors your camp has been fueling regarding my wanting to increase taxes for all the citizens of Paradise Cove."

Dick smiled, but it didn't quite reach his eyes. "Come

off it, Niko. All of America knows that the only way you Democrat and independent types know how to raise money is to increase taxes."

"Do you really think it fair that those in our tax bracket don't share just a bit more of the financial burden for projects that will improve the quality of life in our town? We've been blessed to have more. Giving a bit more should not only be our obligation, but our pleasure."

Dick's eyes slid from Niko to just beyond his shoulder. "Speaking of pleasure, that's a fine filly over there." His voice was barely above a whisper as he slyly ogled Monique. "Too bad she's using that pretty head of hers to compete in a man's world." His eyes slid back to Niko's face, filled with daring.

Niko stayed calm, a huge feat given the fact he wanted to punch Dick in the face. His anger was mixed with a little guilt, though, given the thoughts that had crossed his mind just moments ago.

"Spoken like a true chauvinist," Niko finally answered. "However, I'm sure your female supporters would find this comment revealing, as do I. Someone with these dated, off-putting views has absolutely no place in public office."

"I hear she keeps questionable company, too."

The hairs on the back of Niko's neck stood up. "Oh?"

"That young man she brought here…and the fire."

"Besides the fact that he worked at the school, I don't understand the connection."

"That doesn't surprise me. I don't apologize for upholding the traditions upon which this country was founded. Men were born to lead—women, to follow their leads. Of course, this is just a personal opinion I'm sharing with a friend. My political views are completely different."

"Dick, I've known you half my life. Both of our family roots run deep in Paradise soil. Yes, our families belong to the same clubs, and yes, we've shared lunch a time or two. But make no mistake about it. I am not your friend."

Niko smiled before he walked away. It didn't quite reach his eyes.

Bryce cut him off as he neared the door and followed him into the hallway. "What was that about? Most people wouldn't notice it, but I can tell that the man under that cool veneer is about to explode."

"It's what I get for trying to be friendly with a determined adversary. It was clear Dick was trying to push my buttons."

"Looks like he succeeded. What did he say?"

"Nothing important. Right now, I need to focus. How much time do we have?"

His answer came around the corner as the stage manager neared them. "Places in five minutes, gentlemen," she said to them before going inside the door to inform the other candidates.

Bryce turned to Niko. "Are you sure you're all right?"

"I'm fine. Has our marketing collateral been distributed?"

"There's not a soul in the building who doesn't now have a bumper sticker, Drake for Mayor pamphlet and miniature flag."

"Great."

Both men turned as those inside the room filed out. Niko gave Bryce a nod and fell in beside those heading to the stage.

Minutes later, after the national anthem had been sung and the welcome given, the moderator for the night's debate went over the rules. The irony wasn't lost on Niko that the moderator was not only a woman but a bit of a celebrity. Born and raised in Paradise Cove, she'd graduated college and was now enjoying a stellar career in journalism, most recently as a correspondent for MSNBC. So even though the town boasted just under four thousand people, there was a certain city sophistication to this small-town affair.

"The questions put before you tonight come directly from your constituents," she continued. "They were chosen to cover a wide spectrum of topics and to get to the heart of the matter of why one of you should occupy the office of mayor for this town. I will start to my far right, and thereafter each of you will be given the opportunity to answer. Please keep your comments to two minutes."

After a few more instructions they were ready to begin. Niko had researched and studied well. No topic caught him off guard; the questions were fairly typical regarding education, quality medical care, issues regarding city-owned properties and taxes. As expected, he and Dick came down on opposite sides. Dick basically repeated what he'd said backstage. Niko, however, hadn't shown his hand behind the scenes and, after Monique and Buddy had commented, hit him with a full deck of accurate information.

"It's one thing to quote something incorrectly and another altogether to be blatantly misleading. Mr. Schneider would have you believe that I want to raise everyone's taxes when he knows this is simply not true. I have been very clear in my plans to provide this city with a top-of-the-line educational system, state-of-the-art medical facilities and continued road, sewer and other repairs and other improvements as our city requires. As my grandmother used to tell me, money doesn't grow on trees and neither, Mr. Schneider, will the funds to improve our city. What I've laid out is a fair and straightforward way where every citizen can contribute their equal share, based on their financial ability. If your income falls below a certain amount, you won't be taxed at all. For others, like Mr. Schneider, for instance, and myself, who've been blessed with greater incomes, we will shoulder greater responsibilities. I believe this is only right. I hold fast to that part of our Pledge of Allegiance that says 'to the republic for which it stands, one nation, under God, with liberty and justice for all'!"

He punched the air for emphasis, waving his miniature flag. It could not have been coordinated any better had they rehearsed for days. As one, everyone holding a flag held theirs up and began waving, a sea of flag-holding hands swaying across the stadium. Anyone walking in at this moment would think this election night instead of a debate—one where Niko won!

After quieting the audience, the moderator posed the next question.

"As Paradise Cove continues to grow, the need for affordable housing has become a major issue. While the average median income here is in the six figures, and most are home owners, the growing number of employees hired in service positions need reasonably priced places that can be rented. How would you address this problem? Mr. Schneider, you're up first."

"Paradise Cove prides itself on being one of the most beautiful and friendliest towns in all of Northern California, if not the state. We are also very proud to have one of the lowest crime rates in the country. I believe this is because our town consists of hardworking, God-fearing families who've earned the right to enjoy the life they now have and don't want to worry about an undesirable element moving into the city to rob them of not only their possessions, but their peace of mind. I'd recommend that those seeking rental properties take advantage of the very nice apartment complexes already available within a five-to-ten-mile radius."

Light applause was mixed with a growing murmur

throughout the crowd. Obviously everybody had an opinion on what Dick had just said.

"Thank you, everyone," the moderator said, deftly handling the excited audience. "Quiet, please." Once the noise abated, she turned to Monique. "Ms. Slater?"

"Every city should have affordable housing, period. That Mr. Schneider would suggest otherwise, especially as our population continues to grow and become more diverse, shows he is sorely out of touch with the needs of this town. But I'm not as bothered by that as I am by the presumption that poor people steal or that people who rent care less about their property than home owners. Rather than worrying about an hourly worker who might rob one of his properties, I'd focus on people seeking power by robbing citizens of their basic right to decent houses and stealing their ability to live the American dream."

The applause was spontaneous, with several people standing as they cheered. Throughout the auditorium, miniature American flags were waved back and forth. Even as Niko delighted in Monique's intelligent retort to Dick's tomfoolery, he was also well aware of how she'd just connected with the hearts of those in the room, who were cheering her on with the flags that he'd given them.

All of the loving had almost made Niko forget that Monique was a strong contender. Looking out over the crowd made him remember. With only a couple of months of campaigning remaining, it was time to pull out all the stops. He'd always known better than to underestimate her, but in that moment, it had just gotten real.

Chapter 24

Monique walked into her condo, placing down an armful of campaign stuff and kicking off pumps. She hadn't felt this type of elation from a day's work since arguing her last trial. That had been months ago, and until tonight she hadn't realized how much she missed the drama of the courtroom.

She reached for her phone to dial Niko. It was an automatic thought. Over the past few weeks they'd shared lively conversations on any myriad of subjects. They'd mutually agreed that the upcoming election wouldn't negatively affect them, and for the most part they'd kept to that agreement. As she scrolled for his number, she recalled the scene as she'd left the auditorium: Niko surrounded by friends, family and his throng of supporters.

"Maybe calling now isn't the best idea."

Placing the phone on the counter, Monique decided to fix a cup of tea. As she poured water and decided on her desired herbal mood—Chamomile Calm—she second-guessed her decision to decline invitations by both her godmother and her campaign crew to join them for drinks. At the time, peace and quiet was all she'd longed for. Now, however, in the solitary aftermath of an exciting evening, she was keenly aware of how she missed her family. Under normal circumstances, her parents and brother would have been here with bells on. But a set of heart palpitations had sent her dad to Emergency two days ago. His condition stabilized and nothing serious was found, but the doctor advised bed rest for two days. Understandably, her mother wouldn't leave his side. Her brother, Ian, was in Ecuador, as part of a Doctors Without Borders team. Still, he'd found time to text her an encouraging message. His thoughtfulness made her smile.

While waiting for her tea to steep, she thought of Rob. He would have enjoyed this evening. Belatedly, she wondered whether or not she should have invited him. They didn't talk much by phone these days but had exchanged emails and texts. Reaching for her phone, she punched his number, then put the phone on speaker and sat at the kitchen island as it rang.

"Hello, Rob, it's Monique."

A pause and then "Uh, hi."

Monique frowned. "Did I catch you at a bad time?"

"Yes, I have company. Is something wrong?"

"No, not at all. We had our mayoral debate tonight and I was going to share some of the highlights with you. But no worries…we can talk later."

"Okay, we'll talk later. Goodbye."

"Well, I wasn't expecting that," Monique mumbled as she slid off the bar stool and walked over to dress her tea. Having been broken up for months, it shouldn't have surprised her that Rob was dating. God knew she'd moved on. As she took her cup to the bedroom and prepared for a shower, her heart was happy. Rob was a good man and deserved a woman who loved him. *Maybe,* she thought as she stepped into the shower stall, *our friendship will survive after all.*

A few miles away, at the home of Ike and Jennifer Drake, a small but lively gathering was in full swing. Except for Reginald and Julian, all of Niko's siblings had been at the debate and were now here. Joining them were Bryce and a few other select members of Niko's staff along with his staunchest financial supporters. Their festive mood was proof of how well they'd thought their candidate had performed.

Ike Jr. watched Niko slip into an unoccupied room and close the door. He quickly followed. "Sneaking away for a moment of solitude?"

"I see I'm not going to get it," Niko said with a smile, as he texted on his cell phone.

"How are you holding up?"

"Man, I'm exhausted. But Mom says that as the man of the hour it would be rude to be the first one to leave."

"I'd say she has a point." They laughed. "Things seemed to have gone well tonight. The crowd was fantastic."

"Looked like the whole town showed up. I guess P.C. is ready for change."

"I must say, there was one face I was expecting to see and didn't."

Niko looked up from his phone. "Who?"

"Ashley. Considering her borderline harassment of you lately, I was on the lookout."

"This is one of the biggest events that's happened here lately. She would not have missed it. Trust me, you may not have seen her but I guarantee she was there. Her and her messy mama, too."

"I saw Joy. She was busy shooting daggers at the family while schmoozing up to Dick's wife, Cindy."

Niko slowly shook his head. "Joy's a trip. I almost feel sorry for Ashley. With an opportunistic mother like that, she never had a chance."

"I have to give it to you, little brother. You held it down tonight."

"Thanks, Ike."

"Especially given some of the B.S. being spouted. Dick was in rare form."

"You don't know the half." He shared Dick's earlier comments.

"Doesn't surprise me. He's a part of the old guard who aren't ready to give up their post and realize that times have changed."

"I wanted to punch him in the mouth."

"Yes, I'd feel the same way if someone talked about my woman." Niko voiced a stern denial, which elicited a chuckle from Ike. "You know I'm right. Terrell and I have suspected it for a while. From our keen observations and your reaction just now, I'd say we're right." He looked at Niko for confirmation. A church mouse could not have been quieter.

"I don't know what you're talking about," he finally said.

Ike's smile broadened. "Oh, really? Then you probably don't know why I'm getting bills for services rendered by the cleaning company for the San Francisco condo?" Niko's brow rose ever so slightly. "You forgot that I manage the family expenses and regularly check the books? I know I haven't spent the night there. I could ask Mom and Dad if they've been there recently but—"

"Okay, you've got me. So you can stop looking so smug."

"Don't worry, little brother. Your secret's safe with us. She's definitely the total package—smart, successful, attractive. I can see why you're interested. But I don't need to tell you that you should be very careful."

"No, you don't need to tell me."

"Obviously someone does. If you were sloppy enough that I found out about your tryst, know that others who are watching might catch something, too. The last thing your campaign needs is this to hit the news, and the last thing our family needs is a scandal."

Niko eyed his brother for a moment, then released a deep breath. "Point well taken, Ike. I'll be careful."

"I appreciate careful but I'd much prefer patient. Can you wait until after the election to pursue this relationship?"

"It won't be easy but...I can try."

Ike smiled. "That good, huh?"

"Even better," Niko replied, before heading to the door and out of the room.

Monique tossed and turned, unable to sleep. Even though she'd erased it, Niko's naughty text message continued to play inside her head. It had been weeks since they'd been together and her body was having withdrawals. Back in her college days, her cousins used a phrase when a woman was head over heels for a man. They called her "whipped." Monique could never understand what that meant. Until now. Frustrated, she tossed back the covers and hopped out of bed. At the unexpected sound of her cell phone ringing, she jumped again.

"Niko! You scared me."

"How'd I do that from across town?"

"By calling at this ungodly hour. Do you know what time it is?"

"Time for me to come over and—"

"Don't you dare," she rasped between clenched teeth as she snatched on a robe and proceeded to the kitchen.

"I'm not." Niko's chuckle was low and sexy, causing Monique's resolve to falter. "But I want to."

"Me, too. But it's not going to happen." Monique reached

for a glass and filled it with water before heading back upstairs.

"You're right. We've already been busted."

She froze, barely finding her voice enough to utter, "Who?"

"Relax, sweetheart. Fortunately for us, it was family." He told her what Ike had earlier shared. "He suggested that we take a break until after the election, but *that's* not going to happen."

"I think it's a wise idea."

"Wise, perhaps, but not likely."

"Why not?"

"Did you read the text I sent?"

"Yes."

"Then you know why." His raspy voice caressed her like a breeze, causing her nipples to harden and her walls to contract.

"I can't believe you did that. Of course, it's been deleted. Emails and text messages are like smoking guns."

"How was what I said controversial? Animal lovers would be pleased to learn how much I adore…kitties."

"Ha! You're incorrigible."

"You haven't seen anything yet."

Monique got into bed and snuggled under the cover, wishing that it were Niko instead of her pillow she was hugging right now.

"You were in your element tonight."

"I really enjoyed this evening. The courtroom provides an aspect of it, but I hadn't engaged in a straight-out debate since college."

"You haven't lost your touch. Had the constituents waving their support with flags I'd purchased!"

Monique laughed. "I assumed the city passed those out.

You'll notice I didn't beat you up too badly. Most of my arsenal was saved for Dick. That guy's a piece of work."

"I admit I wanted to punch him earlier."

"Why?"

"Because he was living up to his name. I guess it's to be expected. He's a product of his environment and era, born with a silver spoon, grew up in affluence. What is now patently offensive is probably how he was taught. I wouldn't pay him too much attention."

"As long as his numbers remain low."

"Exactly."

Monique yawned loudly. "Wow, excuse me. That's my cue for sleep time."

"Busy day tomorrow?"

"Yes. Devante is a traffic stop away from going back to jail. I have to do some work on his case. Hopefully I can do all I need from here and not have to fly to L.A."

"You were afraid that he might pick up old habits by going back there."

"Hard to avoid when the other perpetrators are relatives."

"He's lucky to have you in his corner. You're a good woman, Mo Slater."

"Why, thank you, Mr. Drake. For someone running as an independent, you're not bad yourself."

The sound of his laughter as she ended the call was the last thing she heard before drifting off to sleep.

Chapter 25

The following Tuesday at 7:00 a.m., every mayoral candidate assistant was at the *Cove Chronicle* offices, ready to snap up that week's publication. The true yardstick of the past weekend's debate, the latest election polls, were between these pages, and everyone's camp wanted to know how well they did.

Lance was first in line, grabbing his copy and making a beeline to his truck. Within minutes he was at Monique's house, ringing her bell.

"How do we look?" Monique asked as she opened the door. She'd been up since dawn, handling some of her attorney obligations after a heartwarming phone call with her parents.

"I don't know. I came right over."

He handed her the paper. As expected, the article on the mayoral debate was front-page news. The Race Is On! was the story's caption, with the poll numbers front and center, bolded and set apart with a text box.

"Wow! We're closing the gap!" Monique's eyes shone as she sat at the dining-room table and spread out the paper.

Lance joined her. "'Drake, thirty-three percent,'" he read. "'Slater with thirty'! Oh, my goodness, Ms. Mayor... we're only trailing by three percent!" He reached for Monique, pulled her out of the chair and began dancing around the room.

"Okay, Lance, calm down!" Monique demanded, amid a peal of laughter. However, it was hard not to be giddy. Last month they'd trailed Drake by over 10 percent. She returned to where the paper lay and continued to scan the article. "'While Drake remains the front-runner, Slater is gaining ground by obviously drawing supporters from both the independents and Republicans. This is most evident in the decrease in Republican candidate Dick Schneider's numbers, which are down thirteen percent from the poll taken two months ago. Currently, he is carrying twenty-seven percent of the vote while Libertarian candidate Buddy Gao remains at ten percent.'"

"This is great news! We're going to beat them, Mo. We can do it!"

"It's very good news, Lance, but we can't get comfortable. There are still three weeks to go. Anything can happen. So we have to stay focused, keep knocking on doors and passing out flyers, keep calling our constituents and asking for their support. If I'm elected—"

"When you're elected…"

"—there will be plenty enough time to celebrate."

Niko sat at his parents' dining-room table, where at his mother's insistence he'd joined the family for breakfast. Ike had just read aloud the newspaper article on the mayor's race. Everyone had an opinion.

Niko reached for his cup of coffee. "There's no denying it. She was excellent the other night, as I knew she would be. I'm not surprised at the jump in her numbers. But I'm not worried, either."

"Son, I wouldn't be overconfident. I've been reading up on her via the internet and she's quite accomplished."

"Easy on the eyes, too," Terrell added.

"She is rather attractive," Jennifer added, pouring more tea into her cup. "But she's definitely more than a pretty face. Niko, as confident as I am in your skills, I think you may have met your match."

"I never underestimated Monique's abilities. If you'll remember, she was the one who bested me for the championship in a college debate."

Jennifer looked over in surprise. "That's her?"

"Yes. I reminded Dad about it. I thought he'd told you."

"He most certainly did not," Jennifer replied, with a playful slap on her husband's arm. "So she's smart as well as cunning. How interesting." Jennifer's eyes were speculative as she gazed at her son and pondered this news. "I'd like to get to know her. Wonder if she'd accept a dinner invitation."

Niko frowned. "Mom…"

"Now, that would be an interesting meal." Ike Jr.'s eyes were filled with humor as he studied a slightly squirming Niko while taking a drink of juice. "After watching how she handled the debate, I'm tempted to vote for her myself!"

"What y'all need to do is take your focus off of my competition and put it back where it belongs…making these last weeks count. With that being said—" Niko pushed back from the table and stood "—I've got to get to the office." He walked over to his mother and kissed her forehead. "Thanks for breakfast. Terrell, you coming by the campaign office later?"

"Yes, Teresa and I will be there in an hour."

"What's going on at the office?" Ike Sr. asked.

"A plan to ensure that I'll win this election…no matter what."

* * *

Still charged up from the morning's news and a hard but productive twelve-hour day, Monique put on her walking shoes and headed outside. She was just minutes into her power walk when her cell phone rang. She checked the caller ID and slowed down a bit as she answered. "Hey there."

"Counselor!" Niko's voice boomed through her earbuds. "Congratulations on turning this into a real race!"

"Thanks, Niko. I'm thrilled, but needless to say, it's not over until it's over."

"Definitely not, especially since I'm going to do everything in my power to defeat your sexy behind."

"I have no doubt about that."

"Your performance at the debate has definitely garnered its share of attention. You were even the topic at the family breakfast."

"Oh?"

"Ike Jr. said he was tempted to vote for you."

"That's not likely to happen."

"No, but it's a testament to how impressive you were the other night."

"I appreciate that, Niko, and given that we are opponents, I'm impressed with your kindness. It sounds sincere."

"It is." A pause and then "What are your plans for the homestretch?"

"More of the same—canvassing neighborhoods, phone banks, knocking on doors. But I have to go to L.A. to finish handling Devante's case."

"Couldn't get it done from here, huh?"

"No. He violated parole by leaving where I'd placed him and staying with his cousin, a felon. There's a new parole officer. His paperwork got screwed up. It's a mess."

"When are you leaving?"

"Tomorrow."

"How long will you be gone?"

"I'm hoping to be able to finish in a couple days, but it might take a week."

"Okay. Keep in touch."

"I will."

"Turn off the television. Turn off your phone. And get some sleep. You need it."

"You're right. Good night."

Later, as Monique flipped through the channels after packing for her trip, she felt tired but happy. Since moving to Paradise Cove, her life had changed in ways she could not have imagined. Having just broken up with Rob months before coming here, a relationship with Niko had been the last thing on her mind. Sure, when she'd allowed herself to dream, she'd imagined it. But the reality was imminently more amazing.

Reaching over to turn off the bedside lamp, she was surprised to hear someone on television saying her name.

"Monique Slater," the professional yet somber male voice intoned, "running for mayor on a platform that promises Paradise Cove a new day." An intrigued Monique reached for the remote and turned up the volume. "Yet while working as an attorney in Los Angeles, she was fired for improper conduct…dating a client." Monique's mouth dropped, along with the remote from her hand. "Questionable conduct. Questionable character. Questionable acquaintances. Is this the type of person you'd trust to lead you anywhere? I don't think so." As a picture of a mean-looking Monique dissolved into a picturesque view of Paradise Cove, a pleasant female voiceover said, "Paid for by Independent Citizens for a New Paradise."

Independent Citizens? For several seconds she sat there,

stunned. Her hand crept to her chest, heartbeat hammering against it as the words replayed in her head. This couldn't possibly have come from Niko's independent party, she thought. But that was what the ad had said. Grabbing the remote, she punched the guide to see the channel. More shock. The television hadn't been on the town's community station, but on an ABC affiliate.

There had to be an explanation. She got out of bed and placed a call. It rang several times and then went to voice mail. "Niko, it's me. Please call as soon as you get this message." She was about to contact Lance when a comment Niko had made earlier crossed her mind. The force of its implication was chilling.

I'm going to do everything in my power to defeat your sexy behind. "No," Monique muttered, pacing across her bedroom floor. "He wouldn't."

Turn off the television. Turn off your phone.

Words that previously sounded caring now seemed dubious at best. "He didn't want me to see it, wanted me to leave town while this poison spread." No, not possible. She couldn't fathom that someone who had kissed her so tenderly and loved her so completely could possibly stab her in the back. But the thoughts and memories kept coming, particularly snatches of one specific conversation.

Have you ever dated a client?

I was fresh out of law school.

During one of these visits is when things got carried away.

It shouldn't have happened.

I shared some things that I hadn't planned to. I know we're in what's sure to become a highly contested race but—

She called Niko again. No answer. "Calm down, Monique. He always calls back."

After a sleepless night, she headed to the airport. Her godmother, Lance and a couple of workers from the campaign office had seen the commercial and immediately called with their advice and support. She'd phoned Niko several times and left another message. Her calls were not returned.

Chapter 26

Niko paced the room, trying yet again to reach Monique. Since turning on his phone and seeing missed telephone calls and news of the negative ad on her, he'd called repeatedly. He'd worked late and in a rare move decided to turn off his phone and sleep until eight. That was what you got for following your own advice.

Bryce sent him the video link. What he saw was appalling. The words were bad. The images, worse: a laughing Monique and her alleged client/lover leaving the courtroom, a frowning, finger-pointing Monique that Niko figured was taken in a courtroom but out of context looked crazed, and the most disturbing, footage of the recent school fire as the announcer questioned her conduct, character and acquaintances.

He hit Replay. "Paid for by Independent Citizens for a New Paradise." *Who is this?* A name not on any campaign fund lists he'd read, but obviously someone who knew a lot about Monique. Niko hadn't a clue. Aside from her ex Rob, her godmother, Margo, and a best friend named Emma she sometimes mentioned, he didn't know her friends or, in this case, her enemies.

After formulating a strategy, he scrolled the address book for his sister's number. Not only did Teresa freelance for the *Cove Chronicle,* but she was also one of the nosiest people he knew. Teresa could convince a statue to talk. Other sources could have been contacted, but Niko wanted to keep private his involvement in resolving this issue. And that was exactly what he planned to do: help fix this.

"Teresa, good morning."

"Good morning." Niko heard his sister stifle a yawn. "Why are you calling so early?"

"It's not early. It's eight-thirty. Working people should be up by now."

"What do you want?"

"I need you to do a little investigative work."

"Sure, what's up?"

"Have you seen the smear ad on Monique?"

"Mo Slater? No, I haven't."

"I'll email you the link, but it's nasty, sponsored by a group calling themselves the Independent Citizens for a New Paradise."

"This came from your party?"

Niko rubbed his forehead. An uncomfortable thought formed. "I highly doubt it. But your question makes me wonder if that was the intended implication. I need you to query your TV contacts. Find out who submitted the ad and who's connected to this group. I have an idea but need proof. I need this information ASAP."

"I'll get right on it. Send me the video link and give me an hour or two. I'll call back as soon as I have info."

By nine o'clock, Niko was in the office amid constantly ringing phones: associates asking if he'd seen the ad, news reporters wanting a quote. "It's deplorable," he told one reporter. "Anyone who puts out a smear ad like that should have their character questioned."

Despite the unfolding ad drama, Niko had a campaign to spearhead and a business to run. After a couple of interviews and dozens of phone calls, he headed over to Drake

Realty for a business meeting. On the way, his phone rang yet again. It was the call for which he'd waited. He tapped the button on his steering wheel to answer it.

"Monique! I've been calling you all morning."

"Yes, well, I called you all night."

"Babe, so sorry I missed your calls. I turned off my phone, didn't get your messages or see the ad until this morning."

"Had I turned off the television as you suggested, I wouldn't have seen it, either."

"I'm as outraged and angry as I'm sure you are and already working to find out who did it. Their ploy is not going to work."

"Really, Niko? You have no idea who's behind this incident?"

"No. I don't." His brow creased at her choice of words and the sarcastic way they'd been delivered.

"Paid for by the Independent Citizens for a New Paradise—your party. You told me you'd do whatever it took to beat me, but this…"

"Wait, Monique, I—"

"Obviously I am a bad judge of character. My process of choosing friends and lovers is definitely flawed!"

"Monique, I swear to you, I had nothing to do with this."

"That's what I desperately wanted to believe. Yet I can count on one hand without using all my fingers how many people outside my law firm know why I was fired from that job. You took what I shared in confidence and used it to your advantage. Good move, Counselor. I guess all's fair in love, war and political campaigns."

"You've got this all wrong, Monique. And I'm going to prove it."

"What you've proven is that after what happened the

last time we competed, you are willing to do anything to not be defeated again. Was that your M.O. all along? Seduce me, become my friend and confidant and extract information for personal gain?"

"Monique, listen—"

"You're right about one thing. The ploy won't work. I still very much plan to win this race. Goodbye, Niko."

Niko banged a fist on the console. The unthinkable yet plausible reaction he'd feared Monique might have had just been realized.

Monique drove a good five miles before noticing how hard she was gripping the wheel. "Calm down." Easy to say when her life was anything but. Last night she'd doubted Niko's involvement, but by morning he was the only one that made sense. She'd planned to hear him out, but his phony concern was beyond infuriating. He'd help find out the culprit? Yeah, right.

Her eyes became watery. She dared one tear to fall.

Since landing, she'd had a plethora of activities to keep her focused: securing a rental car, picking up Devante, going to the courthouse, meeting with his judge and talking to the family whom Devante would live with. From these visits she surmised that the negative ad wasn't running in Los Angeles and from an earlier conversation with her mother gathered that it hadn't hit the East Coast. She prayed that it wouldn't, that for once the news in Paradise Cove would be like that of most small towns in America... unimportant.

"Who now?" Monique mumbled as her phone rang. She'd received several calls from thirsty reporters. Hopefully this wasn't one. As upset as she was right now, there was no telling what she'd say.

"Emma."

"Hey, Monique. Sorry I missed your call. Spent my morning at the DMV. How are you?"

"I've been better."

"Uh-oh. That's not good."

"Not at all." Monique told Emma what had transpired in the past twenty-four hours. "I was a fool to trust him," she finished, gritting her teeth to stop threatening tears. "He played me like a fiddle and I sang his tune."

"Don't be so hard on yourself, Mo. You took someone at face value, a man you thought you knew. He took advantage of a vulnerable moment. What are you going to do?"

"For starters, get back to Paradise Cove as soon as possible. I had to handle an emergency in L.A., and while here I'd planned to spend some time at the firm. Plans have changed. I can't let an attack like this go unanswered. The longer I take to respond, the more the rumors will spread. I've commented briefly to several reporters, denying the allegations. But that's not enough. I have to go on the air and tell my side."

"Was this televised nationally?"

"No, thank God. I called Mom first thing this morning. If it had run anywhere in their area, believe me, they'd know. It still might get leaked. This story and the fallout from it are going to follow me for the remainder of this campaign."

"I'm so sorry this has happened. Do you have a good support system around you?"

"Yes. Along with raising a whole lot of hell, Margo is also raising the money that will fund this new and unexpected ad. Lance, my campaign manager, has become a good friend who I know has my back."

"What about Rob? I know you guys broke up, but at one time he was a very good friend."

"We talk occasionally, mostly through text and email.

Haven't heard from him lately. I think he's seeing some-one."

"Well, you should call him, get that analytical point of view that people good with numbers are known for."

"Perhaps I will." Monique sighed. "Enough about my soap-opera life. How are you and the baby?"

They chatted for several minutes about cravings and gained weight and phantom contractions. Monique was glad for the diversion. Even if only temporarily, it eased the ache in her heart over Niko's betrayal. She thought about Emma's suggestion to call Rob. It was a good idea. After a trying day in court or a hectic day at the office, his calm, steady demeanor had always calmed her. She'd appreciated different points of view gained from his per-spective. An irony assailed her. If she'd stayed with steady, dependable Rob…none of this would have happened.

Niko, Ike Jr., Warren and Terrell sat around the conference-room table discussing how to handle this latest situation. If one Drake had a problem, they all did.

Ike Jr. eyed his brother. "How are you so sure it's Dick?"

"It has to be him, considering his feelings about women in politics, poor people in our city and an upstart like me having the audacity to run for mayor. This wasn't the work of a Democrat or independent. He did this."

Terrell scowled, crossed his arms. "I think so, too."

"When do you expect to hear back from Teresa?" War-ren asked.

Niko looked at his watch. "By now, I thought. Let me text her."

"I'm ahead of you, bro." Terrell's thumbs flew across the keys.

Ike leaned forward, steepling his fingers on the table. "What are we going to do with whatever proof Teresa finds? Dick isn't foolish enough to have his name connected to something like this. If accused, he'll deny. Then what?"

"Is the story true?" Terrell placed down his phone and looked at Niko. "That's what I want to know."

"She was terminated for an isolated incident, learned her lesson and moved on. We all make mistakes. That shouldn't be held against her or used against her."

Ike Jr. disagreed. "Come on, Niko. This is politics. Any part of her life is fair game."

Niko sprang from his chair. "Are you justifying what happened?"

Ike Jr. stood and looked him in the eye. "I'm saying that if she can't stand the heat, she never should have jumped in the fire."

"Calm down." Warren hadn't raised his voice, yet his tone was authoritative and effective. The men sat. "Let's keep focused on what we're here to do.

"I say we start at the firm where this incident happened, get the names of the attorneys employed during that time and see if there's a connection with Dick."

"That's a start," Terrell replied, once again scrolling and texting on his cell phone. "But the Schneiders know some of everybody. His father was a judge for a hundred years."

"The key is learning just who are the Independent Citizens for a New Paradise." Niko reached for his iPad and opened a screen. "Either that or the corporation that's bankrolling these ads. Commercial slots on major networks are not cheap. Not that money is a factor... Wait." He checked the buzzing cell phone's caller ID. "This is Teresa. What do you have for me, sis?" He listened intently while typing notes. "JDA Associates—that's the corporation?" Terrell opened his mouth to say something, but Niko held up his hand. "Really? That's interesting. Okay, got it. Thanks, sis. If you ever get tired of journalism, I'll hire you as my detective. All right, love you, too."

"What did she find out?" Terrell spoke immediately. "Is it him?"

"The corporation behind this Independent Citizens outfit is called JDA Associates. Anybody heard of them?"

No one had.

"They incorporated recently—I assume to help Dick. In recent weeks, they've made several donations to his campaign."

"That's opinion, Counselor. Conjecture. We need solid proof."

"Okay, Ike. Check this out. After the debate, Schneider's numbers took the biggest hit. He was being bested by a species he feels shouldn't even be in the game. When it comes to that man and this election, circumstantial is all I need."

Ike Jr. nodded, his eyes narrowing in thought. "Let's assume you're right. How can you prove it?"

Niko stood and gathered his things. "Haven't figured that out yet. But I will."

Chapter 27

"That sounds good," Monique said, nodding as she navigated L.A. traffic and headed toward the airport. "I'll write a draft and email it to you on the plane. I have a meeting first thing in the morning with the people securing the airtime, so let's meet around noon. If at all possible, I want this ad to start running tomorrow night."

As she was ending this call, another one came in. Niko. She tapped the ignore button and kept driving. Five minutes later, he called again.

"Niko, please stop calling me. We have nothing to talk about."

"What about the presumption of innocence until guilt is proven?" Silence. "Monique, I'm trying to help you."

"I'll tell you how you can do that. Leave me alone." End of conversation.

Monique took several deep breaths and tried to relax. Hard to do when you thought the man you loved betrayed you. Yes, it was love. As much as she'd tried to deny it, love was the only thing that could hurt this much.

She looked at her watch, noted her surroundings and turned left at the corner. It was a couple of hours till her flight, enough time to grab a to-go order from one of her favorite eateries. This quaint, family-owned Mediterranean establishment was not far from where Rob lived.

Everything was homemade. Their falafels were divine. She found a parking space on the street, hurriedly walked the short distance to the door and stepped inside. Immediately she was assailed with a wonderful fragrance of spices, along with the beautiful smile of the daughter who ran the register.

"Monique! Hello! We haven't seen you in ages."

"It has been a while." Before last night, she would have mentioned that she'd moved to Paradise Cove and was running for mayor. Right now, it felt good to just be Monique, attorney-at-law. "I've missed you guys."

"We've missed you, too. This is for here, right?"

"Actually, no, can we make it to go?"

"Certainly. Your usual?"

"Absolutely."

Monique paid for the meal, then took her drink and sat in the small dining room, separated from the take-out area by colorfully decorated drapes. Having checked only sporadically, she was sure her in-box was filled with unread messages. Head down, she scrolled the screen and had answered several emails when she heard the cashier greet a customer.

"Hey there, Rob!"

He responded cheerfully. "Good afternoon! How are you doing today?"

Rob was here? How perfect a coincidence was that! She'd decided against Emma's suggestion to call him. Looked as though fate had intervened. Smiling, Monique hurriedly placed the cell phone in her purse, grabbed her drink and headed to the counter.

"I thought I heard a familiar voice," she said while rounding the corner.

Rob turned. His eyes widened.

His deer-in-headlights look wasn't what stopped Monique in her tracks. The person standing beside him did the trick.

Well, well, well. Within seconds, she regained her composure and approached with a smile. "Fancy meeting you here!" She leaned in for a hug.

"Hello, Monique." His embrace was lukewarm and brief.

Monique's eyes slid to his lunch date.

"Ashley, we meet again."

"Small world, isn't it?" she said with a smile as fake as her weave.

Monique watched her ex study a menu board he knew by heart. "Rob, can I speak with you for a second?"

Ashley subtly entwined her arm with his. Rob remained silent. Monique's brow arched.

"Now's not a good time," he finally said after clearing his throat. "Why don't you call me later?"

"It will only be a second. I want your opinion on a... project. I'm sure Ashley won't mind."

"Oh, you want to speak with him privately? The way I wanted to speak with Niko when you were around?" Laughing, she turned to the menu.

Rob placed his order. "How long are you in town?"

"Not long."

"Call my office tomorrow. We can talk about your project then."

The server came out with Monique's order. Just as well since Rob's back to her was a fairly clear sign that the talk between them was done. She exited the eatery, thoughts going in a thousand directions. *What is Ashley doing here? With Rob, of all people!* She reached her car and quickly drove off, the delicious falafel all but forgotten. Instead she chewed on what she'd just seen. A situation that required a second opinion. She dialed Lance and told him what had happened.

"What do you make of it?"

"It's definitely interesting." Monique imagined him squinting and rubbing his fingers together as he often did while deep in thought. "How did they meet?"

"I can't imagine the coincidence of their meeting here. It had to have been during his last visit to Paradise Cove. We argued. He left early. Looks like Ashley was somewhere between my house and the airport."

"And you say she's friends with Niko?"

"They used to date, but are just friends now."

"Convenient, wouldn't you say?"

"What do you mean?"

"Your ex comes to P.C., spends a weekend, and weeks later you see Niko's friend all cozy with him."

"I'm not sure I follow." Truth was, she didn't want to.

"Niko met Rob. Niko knows Ashley. Niko's an independent. Connect the dots."

"You think he's behind it?"

"A guy who was leading by more than ten points is now leading by three? With just a couple weeks until the election? Absolutely."

"Do you still think I can win?"

"Absolutely!"

"Good answer. I'm at the car-rental place, and when I get to the airport, I'll be working on the script for tomorrow's shoot. If I need you to come over tonight—"

"Just give me a call."

"Thanks, Lance."

"Don't worry about a thing, Mo. We'll get it done."

Niko sat in his darkened home office, sipping a rare snifter of brandy. It had been a long day. His body was tired. But his mind was wide-awake. Who could have given Dick's people the information on Monique? He rested his head against the office chair, slowly swiveled back and forth. Terrell was right. The Schneider family knew a lot of people. It could be anyone.

Deep in thought, he didn't hear the doorbell. But when it buzzed a second time, he set down his glass and walked to the door. Rare that he had unexpected company. Monique, perhaps? He quickened his steps and looked through the peephole.

"What's up, Terrell?" He glanced at the wall clock. "It's rather late for visiting hours."

"That rule doesn't apply to family." He followed behind Niko.

"Come on back. I'm in the office. Want something to drink?"

"No, I'm good." Terrell plopped into an office chair. "Just left a little birthday bash over at The Groove."

Niko sat and picked up his drink. "Who was celebrating?"

"One of my partner's friends who just moved here from Vegas. He wanted us to show him a little P.C. love."

"Translated, he wanted you to bring some ladies to liven things up."

"Pretty much. I called a few friends and invited them over. One of the girls had something pretty interesting to say. Said she wasn't supposed to tell anybody but, you know, a little alcohol and Drake persuasion…"

Niko lifted the snifter, took a sip and waited.

"Ashley doesn't live here anymore."

"Now, that's a cause for celebration. Sure you don't want a drink?"

Terrell shook his head. "She moved to L.A. with a guy she met here, a dude who was visiting for the weekend."

Niko shrugged. "I'm really not interested in news about Ashley."

"You will be. She's now dating and has moved in with Monique's ex."

"Rob?"

Terrell nodded. "The one we met while having dinner at Acquired Taste."

Both men were quiet as Niko digested this news. "Ike mentioned not seeing Ashley at the debate. But with so many people there that night, I figured he just missed her." Niko stood and paced.

"Are you thinking what I'm thinking?"

"That Rob shared information about Monique with Ashley, who then gave it to Dick? No, Terrell, I can't see that happening. Ash is beautiful, but she's not too bright."

"Perhaps, but she's greedy. And Dick's shrewd. What if he paid her to try to get the goods on Mo?"

"But how would he know about Rob?"

"It's a small town, man. Eyes and ears are everywhere."

Niko returned to his chair and wearily sat down.

"You know Ashley's a charmer. If a man isn't careful, that girl can get anything she wants."

"If Rob is indeed the man she's with, he wouldn't stand a chance."

He reached for his phone and sent Monique a text:

Call ASAP re Rob, Ashley and how your story got leaked.

Lance had left and she was basically satisfied with what they'd worked out. Still, before she sent the final copy to her PR manager, Monique decided to read the script aloud one final time:

"'Years ago, while working as an intern at my very first law firm, I made an unwise choice, developing a friendship with a young man while working his case. I was young. He was scared. And alone. I brought personal feelings into a professional situation. This mistake cost me my job, but not my integrity. A hard knock, but a lesson learned. I'm a better person for it.

"'Recently my conduct, character and choice of acquaintances have been called into question. I am disappointed that someone felt it necessary to use unscrupulous tactics to sully my name and forward their agenda. Because I am a woman of character, I will not respond in kind. I will continue to be who I've always been—the person who wants to move beyond smear tactics and innuendo and help lead the citizens of Paradise Cove into a new day. I am Monique Slater, and I approve this message.'"

She sent off the email and, after turning off her laptop, climbed the stairs to her bedroom. With the adrenaline of anger wearing off, exhaustion crept in to replace it. Mind, body, spirit—every part of her was tired. All she wanted to do was take a hot shower and crawl into bed.

Shoot! I forgot to tell Lance where to meet us in the morning. She reached for her phone to send him a text. Instead, she read the one from Niko…twice, and then again. *He thinks Rob outed me?* "That's ridiculous. Rob would never do that." *Would he?*

She sat on the bed, remembering the L.A. run-in and how nervous and out of character Rob had acted. But the Rob she knew would never participate in tarnishing her image. Until today, the Rob she knew would not date someone like Ashley, either.

She snatched the phone off the bed and dialed his number. It went to voice mail. "Rob, this is Monique. We need to speak as soon as possible. No matter the time, when you get this message, call me."

Reenergized, she scrolled to another number. Then, on

second thought, she placed the phone on a nightstand and headed to her closet. The conversation with Niko had to be face-to-face.

Chapter 28

Terrell had barely been gone thirty minutes when Niko's doorbell rang again. He'd just stepped out of the shower.

"What did he forget?" Niko mumbled. He reached for a towel, wrapping it around himself as he padded barefoot down the stairs and to the door. "Man, you'd forget your head…" The rest of the sentence died on his lips. "Monique."

She immediately noticed his state of undress. "I'm sorry to come over without calling, and I hope I didn't disturb you. But I had to talk to you, in person. It couldn't wait."

He nodded. "Come in." They walked into his living room. Niko sat on the couch, just as comfortably as he would if fully dressed. He motioned for Monique to sit, as well. She chose an accent chair across from him.

"I take it you read my text and finally decided that you might need to listen to what I have to say."

"Yes."

"Good. The first thing you need to hear and understand is that neither I nor my independent party is behind that ad."

"I've begun to entertain other possibilities."

"I understand you were angry, with every right to be upset. But I'm offended that you would think so little of me as to rush to judgment and declare me guilty without so much as a conversation. Even an admitted murderer is entitled to a fair trial."

"You're right. I should have listened."

"I'm sure mentioning Rob and Ashley in the same sentence got your attention. Rumor has it they're together, living in L.A."

"It's not a rumor."

"You knew about this?"

"I ran into them today." Niko's brow arched. "On my way to the airport, I stopped to grab a bite to eat at one of my favorite spots. The place just so happens to be near Rob's house and also just so happens to be one of his favorite places, too. So, I'm sitting in the dining room waiting for my order when I hear him being greeted as he walked through the door."

"He didn't see you?"

"There's a curtain that separates the rooms."

"What happened?"

She told him. "He acted strangely," she finished. "But given that he was with someone new and we used to date, that's not unusual. The weird part was Ashley. Rob hardly seems her type."

The tension was palpable as silence descended. "How did you find out about them?" she finally asked.

"My brother told me. He ran into one of Ashley's friends at a party, who mentioned she'd met a guy from L.A. a while back and he'd asked her to move in."

"That is so unlike him! Rob is a methodical, deliberate thinker who never makes a spontaneous move. That he just met a woman who is now living with him is… mind-boggling!" Unable to sit still, she stood and looked out the window.

"Does he know about what happened when you were an intern?"

She turned, crossing her arms as she looked at him. "Yes."

"Then I'd bet my life that he told Ashley, and she told someone who either gave or sold the information to Schneider."

"You sound sure of it."

"A company called JDA Associates paid for the ad. They've also made several contributions to Dick's campaign. I just have to find out their names."

Niko's phone buzzed. Monique gave him a look. *She thinks it's a booty call.* He tapped the speaker button.

"What's going on, sis? No, I'm still up." He casually observed Monique taking her seat again while he listened. "You sure about this?"

Her mouth fell open.

"Well, I'll be damned. Thanks to you, Teresa, the question I just brought up has been answered."

He ended the call and stared at Monique.

"Joy and Ashley?" She could barely hear her voice through the shock. "The DeWitts are behind the ad?"

"You heard it for yourself. J-D-A. Joy. DeWitt. Ashley. Seems obvious now, though I never would have guessed."

"I can't believe it."

"I can. You don't know Joy. And Ashley is a chip off the old block."

"Which can only mean one thing." Her shoulders fell. "Rob told Ashley."

"And she told Joy."

For the first time since opening the door, his mask slipped, giving Monique a brief look at the hurt in his eyes. It moved her off the chair and to the couch.

"Niko, I'm sorry. You're right. I heard Independent Citizens and immediately found you guilty. I was too angry to listen, too hurt at the thought that you could betray me."

"So you can imagine how your accusations made me feel."

"Yes." She reached out to touch him.

He stayed her hand. "Don't." He stood and increased the distance between them.

"Like I said earlier, you had every right to be upset. Unfortunately, words once spoken cannot be unsaid.

"With everything we've shared—the days of conversation and nights making love—how could you flip the switch so quickly and believe me to be the type of man who'd ruin your reputation?"

She stood. He tensed. She did not walk toward him. "I should have considered how great of a man you are and listened the first time you called. But I misread the fact that I couldn't reach you. By the time you called, I'd made up my mind. You did it. End of story. I overreacted, spoke without thinking and made terrible accusations. Niko, I'm sorry. Can you forgive me?"

"I can forgive you but I won't forget."

"You and I have shared amazing times together. I'd hate to lose our friendship."

"I can't make any promises on that front. What I can do is share my thoughts on the matter and voice my outrage. Short of endorsing you, that's about it."

She was the only one who smiled.

"I appreciate that, Niko. Tomorrow I'm taping my response to that horrible ad. Hopefully, it will air tomorrow night."

"I'll be watching."

Two seconds passed.

Five.

Ten.

Niko stood feet away, arms crossed, his expression once

again unreadable. "It's late, and we both have busy days tomorrow."

"You're right." Monique reached for her purse. "Thanks for seeing me, Niko."

"Teresa's call was right on time." He walked to the door and opened it. "See you later, Monique."

She paused, uncertain. He did not look at her. "Okay, then. Good night."

Monique walked to the car with a heavy heart. For a moment she just sat there, as regret mixed with sadness and filled her soul. As an attorney, she'd always prided herself on being meticulous in her fact gathering, diligent in her research. Where had that discipline been when she'd seen the ad?

There was not one thing Niko had said that hadn't been accurate. She should have known that he'd never do anything like this to her. At the very least, he should have been given the benefit of the doubt. But that hadn't happened. And now, Monique realized as she started the car and headed back to her condo, it may be too late to get back what they had.

The next day went by in a blur: meetings, the taping, more meetings, an appearance at the local grocery store and still more meetings. Monique welcomed the nonstop pace. It helped her forget how sexy Niko had looked in that towel last night, how much she'd wanted to feel his embrace and, most of all, the hurt she'd seen in his soulful brown eyes. By the time she joined her staff for dinner at the Cove Café, she'd almost put last night out of her mind. What couldn't be forgotten, however, was that almost everyone in P.C. had seen the negative ad, evidenced by the myriad of looks she now received. She forged ahead, greeted everyone with a smile and invited them to hear the other side of the story, airing tonight on their local news.

"What time is it?" her volunteer coordinator asked.

Lance looked at his watch. "Almost eight o'clock." He looked at Monique. "Are you sure you don't want to watch it? We can make it to my house in time."

Monique shook her head. "I've watched it a dozen times already. I did my best and told the truth. It's now up to the citizens to decide who they'll believe."

The first response came about fifteen minutes later, as they were finishing their meal. A middle-aged woman who Monique remembered worked at the grocery store walked up to their table.

"I just wanted to tell you that I saw your ad. And while it's nobody's business who you dated, I applaud your honesty. Who hasn't done something in their youth that they've later regretted? Hold your head up, darlin'. You've still got my vote."

Monique stood and hugged her. "Thank you very much. I truly appreciate your support."

These sincere words warmed her heart, but not near as much as the text she received on the way home. It was from Niko and said simply: Good job.

Niko buried himself in work. A week after seeing her, he continued to nurse a bruised ego and tamp down anger at her misjudgment of his character. Even so, he missed Monique more than he'd imagined. She'd wanted him that night; he was sure of it. Probably only half as much as he'd wanted her. The look of raw desire in her eyes when she'd tried to touch him had almost been his undoing.

Bryce entered the office. "I'll be glad when this is over," he lamented, as he sat down with a sigh. "You're a slave driver."

"Ha! You want this as much as I do."

"What I want is to be city commissioner."

"Once I'm elected, you've got it."

"After that initial dip, her numbers have increased and are now holding steady. Schneider has lost three more points."

"Yes, and probably to Monique. Instead of running from the situation, she tackled it head-on. Her response was perfect, forthright, succinct and genuine. Those are the qualities people want to see in their leaders."

Niko's intercom buzzed. "Yes?"

"Lawrence Hayes, the principal of P.C. Elementary, is on line one."

"Thanks."

Niko took the call, finished his day and had dinner with his family. With one week left in the final stretch, it would be the last meal he enjoyed with them until after the election.

"Emma, I need to take this call. Let's catch up again soon, okay?" Monique tapped her cell-phone screen and placed the call on speaker as she prepared a cup of tea. "Hello?"

"Monique, it's me."

"Hello, Devante. I've been meaning to call you."

"I know you've been busy, trying to become a big-shot mayor and whatnot. It's about that time, right?"

"Yes, a week until election day. One way or another, it's the end of the race."

"How are you feeling?"

"I'm okay. I've worked hard and done my best. Now it's up to the voters. How are you doing?"

"Great! In fact, that's why I called—to thank you."

Monique stopped in midstir. "Thank me? For what?"

"For whatever you did to get Mr. Hayes to call and

offer me my old job back. The chief of police there called me, too."

"Devante, I'm thrilled that Lawrence called you, but I haven't spoken with him."

"Oh, I just assumed you were the reason he called because of how he talked, about wanting to help me turn my life around and stay positive. He's talked to my parole officer and everything. I'm going to move back there and take online classes. After I get my degree, he'll promote me to the athletic department."

Monique picked up the phone and walked to the couch. "This is wonderful news. I bet Lawrence realized what a gem of a person he'd lost. I know the kids loved you. They probably hounded him to hire you back."

"Ha! That sounds about right."

"Why did the chief of police call you?"

"To explain how by investigating me he was only following standard procedure, blah, blah, blah, and to tell me I was welcome in his town."

"Really?"

"Yeah, I thought that was kind of weird. Definitely sounded like you worked that."

"Nope, haven't talked to him, either. So when are you coming back, and do you need a place to stay?"

"That's the other thing. Mr. Hayes's nephew has a three-bedroom condo and is looking for a roommate. I'll move in about two weeks."

"Just to be sure there are no more problems, I'll call your parole officer first thing in the morning."

"Call him after you're elected mayor. That will sound more official, and let him know I'm rolling with the ballers."

"Thanks for that vote of confidence. I'll see you soon."

Monique sipped tea and thought about the call. What

happened to bring about Lawrence's change of heart? And the police chief calling? *What would make him do that?*

As days went by, the question changed. It became not what…but who?

The night before the election, Monique called Niko. They hadn't talked since the night she'd gone to his house. She hoped he'd answer. That he wasn't busy. Or with someone else.

"Hello?"

"Niko, it's Monique." Silence. "I won't keep you, just called to thank you for what you did for Devante. You are the one who talked to Lawrence, correct?"

"I made a couple calls. No big deal."

"It's a very big deal. He's superexcited to come back, and that the chief of police welcomed him personally? That type of behavior from law enforcement is something that men like Devante rarely see."

"From what you've told me, I felt he deserved a chance."

"He does. Thank you."

"You're welcome."

She settled back on the couch with a huge grin on her face. Simply talking to a man shouldn't make her this happy. But it did. "So…are you ready for tomorrow night?"

"Yes. Are you?"

"I guess so. Still working, though." She waited, but he said nothing further. The ice may have thawed a bit, but it hadn't melted. "Well, I'll let you go, then. Good luck, Niko."

"You, too, Monique. Goodbye."

Ending the call on this election eve, she came to a painful truth: she'd gladly give up being mayor to get back her man.

Chapter 29

Monique sat in the hotel suite with Margo, Lance, his partner and her parents. The results were coming in, and with 70 percent of the votes in, things did not look good.

Mrs. Slater looked over at her daughter's forlorn face. "It's okay, Monique. You ran a clean race and did your best. That's all we can ask for."

"It's not over yet." George's eyes remained glued to the TV screen. "He's only ahead by five percent. Thirty percent of the vote has not been counted. Anything can happen."

"Dad, you're an eternal optimist."

Lance looked at Monique. "I'm with your dad."

"We're all very proud of you," Margo said, muting the television during a commercial break. "You withstood a nasty scandal with strong character and grace. You turned a sour lemon into sweet lemonade. Sharing your story was inspiring. It's not the act of falling, but getting up that counts. You were sincere and honest. That resonated, and not just with women voters."

Lance reached for the remote. "It's back on!" Monique rose and paced as she watched the anchors pontificate on the election and its possible results.

"She did well," the male anchor was saying as she stood

with toe tapping. "Especially given the scandal that midway through rocked her campaign."

"But she went up against a Drake," the female anchor countered. "Given the number of homes they've built, businesses they've helped and charities they've funded, they're like royalty in Paradise Cove."

Monique slowly shook her head. "I guess that says it all."

Margo eyed her watch. "How long do you think it will be before they call the race?"

"Probably another hour," Monique replied. "Really, Margo, I know it's late. You've been so supportive, but I can have Lance drive you home."

"I wouldn't think of leaving. I want to be one of the first to hug our city's new mayor."

"In that case," Monique answered sarcastically, "you may want to go join Niko at the country club."

Or not. Contrary to what Monique believed, Niko was not inside watching the election results. He wasn't even near a television. He and his brothers were enjoying an impromptu pickup game, sweating hard and talking trash about who could do what on the basketball court.

"It's been a while, son," Terrell said to their eldest brother, Ike Jr. "I'll try not to whip that butt too bad."

Ike Jr. looked at Julian, who'd arrived from the East Coast just hours ago. "Said to the man who taught all of y'all how to play the game." To make his point, he faked left, moved right and scored an easy layup.

"Come on, man," Niko admonished Terrell, his two-on-two teammate. "Stop jaw-jacking and play ball." He caught the ball from Ike Jr. and passed it on.

Terrell took the ball and started bouncing it. "Don't

worry, bro. We don't intend to let you lose nothing to-night."

All heads turned as Terrell's twin, Teresa, came rush-ing around the back of Niko's house, where the basketball court was located. "Niko! Are you crazy? Why are you standing there in sweaty shorts instead of a suit?"

Niko stopped. "What time is it?"

"Time for you to get a clue! Don't you know you'll need to make your speech? You'd better get changed and get over to the club now! Bryce has been calling you for the last fifteen minutes and is about to blow a gasket."

Niko threw the ball to Ike Jr. and reached for a towel. "And here I thought y'all had my back. I'm getting ready to have to make a speech on television wearing a sweaty T-shirt."

Thirty minutes later and no one would have dreamed that Niko had just spent an hour playing with his brothers on the basketball court. He walked into the country club as if he'd just left a magazine-cover photo shoot. His double-breasted navy suit fit his frame to a T and the baby-blue shirt paired well with the red, white and blue polka-dot tie. A small flag pin was clipped to his lapel, with a plati-num watch and matching cuff links and tie pin his only other accessories. That and his winning smile.

He entered through the back and walked to the private room where his family, staff and financial donors were seated. "Good evening, everyone. My apologies for being late. I had to quickly kick my brothers' butts on the bas-ketball court."

This quip caused a flurry of responses and laughter across the room.

His mother walked over. "You'll likely miss your own funeral," she softly chided, while accepting a kiss on the cheek. "Spending time with your brothers was obviously beneficial. You look relaxed."

"I am." He looked up as Bryce headed his way. "Mom, if you'll excuse me." And then to Bryce, "I know. I owe you. Lost track of time."

"Fortunately for you it doesn't matter. Your lead is increasing. They'll probably call the election any minute. Let's head over to the city auditorium, where your public awaits."

Niko turned to the room. "Before we leave, I just want to thank everyone for all your hard work. I couldn't have done this without you."

"Make sure you have your badges," Bryce added. "You'll need them to enter the section that's reserved for Drake VIPs."

On the way over, Niko's phone rang. "Hello, Monique." He held up his hand for quiet. "Thank you." Nodding, he continued. "We both worked hard. In spite of everything that happened, you ran an excellent campaign. I really mean that."

Bryce looked over. "She conceded?"

Niko nodded.

Terrell's thumbs flew across his iPhone, not slowing down even while talking. "She's a classy lady. If Niko hadn't been running, she would have gotten my vote."

"I've seen those appreciative looks you've given her. Not so sure she didn't get it anyway."

"It was a hard decision, but in the end…family first."

"Has Dick called?"

Niko glanced at his dad to see if he was kidding. "I don't expect to hear from him—not tonight."

Ike Sr. shook his head. "He'll call. It's part of the tradition, and Dick holds firm to that."

They reached city hall. A large crowd had gathered

and spilled onto the sidewalk. Signs and placards were everywhere. As soon as Niko stepped out of the car, the chants began.

"Mayor Drake! Mayor Drake!"

He entered the fray, shaking the hands of those who lined the sidewalk. Anyone watching would have figured Niko a seasoned politician and not a first-time official. Inside, the noise was explosive: people cheering, whistles blowing, the band playing a lively tune. Later, he'd swear that the nearly four thousand citizens in Paradise Cove had all turned out to hear his victory speech. It took a while, but finally he made it to the stage. Standing there was one of the town's wealthiest businessmen, who, along with being president of the chamber of commerce and a staunch supporter, had turned into a valuable friend. They shook hands and hugged before Bryce approached the microphone on the podium. He raised his hands and after a while the hall quieted. "Ladies and gentlemen, I present to you the newly elected mayor of Paradise Cove…Nicodemus 'Niko' Drake!"

Chapter 30

She'd just stepped out of the shower when she heard it. The doorbell. Looking at the clock, she figured she'd imagined it. Who would be coming to see her at 1:00 a.m.? But there it was again, a ring followed by a knock. Seconds later, her phone began to ring. What was going on? She hurried over to the nightstand in her master bedroom to retrieve the phone.

"Niko?"

"Please let me in. I've only been mayor for a few hours, way too soon to make front-page news." Monique grabbed a robe and hurried downstairs. She opened the door and immediately found herself wrapped in Niko's embrace.

They stepped inside. "I'd thought you'd be celebrating at the club."

"They're still there. But I wanted to have a different kind of party."

"You are absolutely insane to be standing in my living room. But I'm so glad you're here."

She hugged him, relishing the body she'd missed so much. He embraced her just as fervently, and touches became kisses—hot, wet, thorough—before both stopped to catch their breath.

Niko pushed an errant strand of hair away from her face. "I've missed you."

"I've missed you, too."

Monique noted how Niko's eyes traveled the length of her body. She became aware that the silk robe she'd snatched from the foot of her bed now clung to her partially wet skin; the thrill from his touch had hardened her nipples.

"I just got out of the shower," she stuttered.

"Figured as much" was his soft reply as he visibly swallowed.

"Um…would you like to sit down? I could make tea."

"Actually, I brought this." Niko pulled out a bottle of pricey bubbly from Drake Wines and Resort, his Southern California cousin's thriving winery.

Niko's unexpected presence had Monique so flustered she'd not even noticed the wine bag hanging from his wrist. "Why, of course. It is a night of celebration."

"Monique, I know you wanted to win…"

"No." She held up her hand. "Really, there is no need for apologies. Earlier when I called to congratulate you, Niko, I meant it. Yours was a hard-fought campaign and you deserve the victory."

"It didn't feel complete until now. We went through it together."

"That we did. It was quite the experience. But the election is over. It's time for me to reorganize my life."

"I hope that doesn't include your leaving Paradise Cove."

"Why wouldn't I?"

"Because after all the drama with Ashley and Rob and elections and scandals…I'm still crazy about you?"

"We've shared some special moments."

"For me it was that…" Niko took a step toward her, love radiating from his pores. "And so much more."

Monique took a breath, trying to slow her rapidly beating heart. She'd longed for this moment, never thinking it would come true. But he was here. And he wanted her.

She stepped into his open arms. For several moments there was only silence, save the sound of their hearts beating in perfect synchronicity. When he stepped back to look at her, he saw tears in her eyes. "Baby, what is it? What's wrong?"

"Nothing." Her dazzling smile showed through the tears. "Everything's right. This feels so right, Niko. And I'm so happy for you."

"I'm happy for us. Tonight, no one in the world can be happier than me."

Slowly, their eyes locked on each other, he lowered his head. At first the kiss was soft, tentative. He lightly brushed his lips against hers before lifting his head ever so slightly to kiss the tip of her nose and the eyelids that had just fluttered closed. Taking his time, he moved to kiss her temple, then lowered his head back down to claim her mouth, this time thoroughly and possessively, leaving no part of her luscious lips untouched.

Monique was drowning in desire. She'd never said it aloud, but her heart felt it. She was head over heels in love with this man. Now she could admit it, at least to herself. Because for the first time she felt there was a real chance that he loved her, too. It made her swoon with happiness and wet with the need to consummate this truth.

Niko stepped back, removed his suit coat. His eyes never left her as he undressed right there, in the living room. She looked down and unconsciously licked her lips. His dick was hard and ready. Her body responded, sticky dew on her feminine flower. She untied the robe. It slid to the floor.

He was there almost before it landed. On bended knee, his tongue caressing her heat, outlining her folds as he suckled her love button. She gasped, spreading her legs and gripping his shoulders. He moved them to the couch, laid her down and continued to feast. He kissed, licked, loved every inch of her—no part of her body was left untouched.

And when he was done, she returned the favor.

"I want you inside me." Her whisper was frantic, urgent.

"That's exactly where I want to be." He steadied her on the couch, entered from behind. His hands glided possessively over her tush as he plunged in—quickly, deeply—touching her core, searing his name across her heart. He set up a rhythm, slow and methodical. Tweaking her nipples, licking her earlobes, playing her body. It was a beautiful tune. Over and again, he thrust himself into her warmth. And still, it was not enough. He didn't want to stop.

And from the way she flipped the script, pushed him down, sat astride and began riding, Monique wasn't quite ready to end things, either.

After multiple climaxes, the two cuddled beneath Monique's afghan throw.

"Is this the party you were looking for?"

He kissed her temple. "Indeed. This is exactly how I wanted to celebrate."

"Sounds like the perfect time for champagne."

Monique got up and strode naked into the kitchen. Niko followed close behind, admiring the shape of her butt and the sway of her body. She reached for two champagne flutes while Niko uncorked the bottle.

She joined him at the island, examining the bottle before she poured. "I don't think I've seen this at the wine store."

"This isn't sold in Warren's store. It's an exclusive, limited-edition line sold mostly to high-end restaurants and hotels. It's called Diamond…fine, rare, bubbly, valuable…just like you."

"That's very sweet. Thank you." She poured an equal amount into both glasses and gave one to Niko.

He kissed her nose. "What are we toasting to?"

"Your victory, of course."

"I'll drink to that and to what can happen between us now that the race is over."

"Okay," she said with raised brow. "To us and whatever comes next."

Chapter 31

February, Three Months Later

Niko and Monique arrived at the country club and parked next to the private dining-room entrance. "Are you ready for our engagement party, Mrs. Drake?"

"The operative word is *engagement*," Monique said with a smile. "Technically, I'm still Ms. Slater."

Niko leaned toward her, his eyes darkening with desire. "To hell with technicalities." His lips pressed against hers, soft and warm, before he brushed his tongue across the crease of her lips to deepen the exchange.

"You're ruining my lipstick," Monique murmured, before dipping her tongue back into Niko's warm mouth for seconds and thirds.

"To hell with that, too. In fact, why don't we bypass all this hoopla and go back to the house? I haven't had you for a few hours and my body is feeling the loss."

"These three months will pass in the blink of an eye, and come June, you'll have me for the rest of your life."

The outer door to the private dining room opened. Out walked Warren and his cousin Dexter. They headed straight to Niko's car, in spite of the fact that they could see he was busy. Warren knocked on the window. "Get a room!" he shouted.

"Mind your business!" Niko shouted back.

Monique laughed, pulled out her compact and repaired her lipstick.

Once they'd exited the car, Niko asked Warren, "How'd you know I was out here?"

"We didn't. Came out so I could show Dexter my new truck."

Niko shook his head. Since buying a ranch and marrying his neighbor, a bona fide cowgirl, Warren had totally embraced the country life, complete with Stetson and boots. "You Ford tough now?"

"Naw, I'm a Dodge man. Charli has the Ford."

"I'll see your truck after the festivities," Dexter said, placing his arm around Monique. "Now it's time to toast the prettiest girl in the room."

"You've got that right," Niko said.

"Besides my wife," Dexter added.

The four of them entered the private dining room. Warren and Dexter stepped aside as the room stood and applauded the night's special guests. Niko and Monique walked to the front, center table occupied by their parents. They hugged Ike and Jennifer before turning to Monique's parents, Caroline and George.

"You look stunning," Caroline said, her eyes tearing up as she hugged her daughter. "Silver is a perfect complement to your skin tone. It's different, but I think your wedding colors of silver with shades of pink are going to be stunning." She turned to Niko, who'd just shaken hands with George. "Hello, handsome," she said, hugging her future son-in-law. "My daughter is simply beaming," she whispered. "And it's all because of you."

"Excuse me—may I have your attention please?" Everyone turned to see Ike Jr. at the microphone. "Please help me welcome Niko Drake, the mayor of Paradise Cove, and Monique Slater, the beautiful first lady who raced him into office!"

"Now he's racing her to the altar!" someone shouted.

The festivities were under way.

For the next hour, Niko and Monique made their way around the room. After talking to her brother and his wife, they greeted the rest of the one hundred and fifty guests that included Niko's extended family from Southern California and New Orleans, Monique's good friend Emma and her husband, their colleagues from the legal world and the citizens of Paradise Cove who'd known Niko a lifetime and had warmly welcomed his fiancée. When they reached Margo, both Monique and Niko gave her a special hug. It was her prodding to keep a promise that had brought Monique to Paradise Cove.

"I'm so happy for you, darling," Margo said. "Happy for you both. Do you have a designer for your wedding gown?"

"Not yet. We're looking."

"Call me next week. I know someone in Los Angeles who could design a masterpiece."

"Will do."

Having circled the room, they arrived back at the table they'd share with their parents and married siblings. Ike immediately stood to offer a toast.

"We'd like to thank all of you for coming to celebrate the engagement of my son Nicodemus to his lovely fiancée, Monique. Niko has always been adventurous, some might even say a hellion." Laughter caused him to pause. "At times the wife and I wondered whether there would ever be someone to tame him. But in Monique, he's met his match both intellectually and academically, in mind, body and spirit. She comes from a great family, one which we are proud to align with." He turned to Monique. "Welcome to the family, dear." Raising his glass, he ended, "to Niko and Monique!"

"Hear, hear!"

After a couple more toasts, Emma stood. "Monique, from the time we met in college, I knew you were special. And I knew it would take a special man to win your heart. You are a great professional, a great career woman. But I think you will be an even greater wife and mother."

At the sound of the *M* word, Monique feigned coughing, which elicited a big laugh from the crowd. The serving began and lively conversation filled the room. Beneath their table, Niko squeezed Monique's thigh. Months later his touch, his scent, his smile, his presence still caused her muscles to constrict and kitty to moisten. Tonight was no different.

"Behave," she gritted out between a smile.

"Not a chance," he replied, giving her thigh another squeeze followed by a kiss on her temple. "In fact, when I get you back to my house…there's going to be a whole lot of misbehaving."

Monique felt the heat rise from her chest to her ears. She dared not raise her eyes, sure that anyone looking at her would be able to tell what was on her mind. Niko was insatiable and his comment had brought to mind what had occurred that very morning. Until now, her lovemaking experience had been fairly standard, pretty routine. But with Niko, lovemaking was an adventure. Just this morning he'd come to bed with warm caramel. Remembering that sticky substance on her thighs and Niko licking it off caused her to shudder.

She was happy when a few minutes later she caught Emma's eye and signaled her to meet in the bathroom.

"Excuse me," she said to the table as she rose. "I'll be right back." The men stood as well until she left the table.

"Do you need any help?" her sister-in-law asked.

"No, I'm fine. Thanks." She held her smile until she turned the corner. "My feet are killing me," she whispered to Emma as soon as they'd turned the corner and were out of sight from the room. "And my face is sore from smiling. I'm thrilled to be becoming Niko's missus, but I'm not sure I'll survive the hoopla!"

"You look beautiful," Emma reassured her. "And you'll be fine."

"You're the one who looks amazing. No one would guess that you had little Amelia just two months ago!"

They reached the bathroom. Monique pulled out her compact and patted her face.

She turned to Emma, glad that with her upcoming nuptials their friendship had deepened. "I'm glad we got a moment alone. I wanted to thank you."

"For what?"

"For giving advice that I didn't ask for. Do you remember?"

"Mo, we have a newborn. I get no sleep and these days am lucky to remember my name."

"It was just after clinching the Democratic nomination. With Niko, I was determined to keep my distance. But you told me to take a chance, that if I saw something I wanted, to go for it. And now I'm wearing his ring."

Emma grabbed several tissues. "Oh, look at you getting all sentimental and making me cry." She gave some to Monique, who dabbed her eyes. "My hormones are still all over the place. It doesn't take much." She tossed her tissue in the wastebasket. "Now, let's hear the good stuff."

"About what?"

"Your love life, silly. Is he any good in bed?"

"Em!"

"Hey, this is important. A very serious matter!"

"Yes, it is, and he's amazing. Sometimes I think he's almost too much."

"Ah." Emma's eyes sparkled. "Trust me, that's a good thing. My husband and I have never had a disagreement that a good swiving didn't fix."

"Swiving? Seriously?"

"I'm a historical-romance fiend. Don't judge me."

Monique laughed. "I won't. I'll just think of you the next time I get my swive on." She took a deep breath. "Okay, I think I'm ready to face the table again. Niko keeps whispering nasty comments to me. I can barely look my parents or in-laws in the eye!"

"Just visualize what they had to do to get you here and you'll be fine."

"Ugh!"

"Ha! At least you're not thinking of Niko's comments right now."

"I only wish I were!" She grabbed her friend and hugged her. "Thanks for everything. Love you, Em."

"Love you, Mo."

They returned to their tables. Niko took up where he'd left off, leaning toward her and whispering, "I missed you," before surreptitiously licking her ear.

Her gasp caused the table to turn in her direction. "Is everything all right, dear?" her father asked.

"Yes." *It would be even better if I could control my heartbeat.*

Warren's wife, Charli, took in Monique's flushed color. Being married to Niko's brother, she had an idea why. It was time to shift the table's focus. "Monique, I love your color scheme. What made you choose them?"

"Thank you," she said, her eyes conveying that the gratitude was not only for the compliment but for the question. "Pink has always been my favorite color. The idea of silver came from the Silver Serenade Concert. It was a very special night." She glanced at Niko and saw his knowing smile. Reaching beneath the table, she squeezed his hand and with a quick shake of her head dared him to comment further. Everyone knew about the concert's success but only she and Niko knew that trip to San Francisco's true significance, when magic had happened and their lives had changed. That special moment would remain just between the two of them. For Niko and Monique it was the start of it all…their secret silver night.

* * * * *

Can he convince her to take another chance on love?

ESSENCE **BESTSELLING AUTHOR**

GWYNNE FORSTER

MCNEIL'S *MATCH*

After a bitter divorce, twenty-nine-year-old Lynne Thurston is faced with the prospect of not knowing what to do with the rest of her life. Once a highly ranked pro tennis player, she gave it all up six years ago when she got married. Now with nothing else to lose, can she make a comeback on the tennis circuit? Sloan McNeil is a businessman who wants to convince Lynne that she still has what it takes… both on *and* off the court!

"Caring and sensitive…FLYING HIGH is a moving story fit for any keeper shelf."
—*RT Book Reviews*

Available September 2014 wherever books are sold!

REQUEST YOUR FREE BOOKS!

2 FREE NOVELS
PLUS 2 FREE GIFTS!

KIMANI™
ROMANCE

Love's ultimate destination!

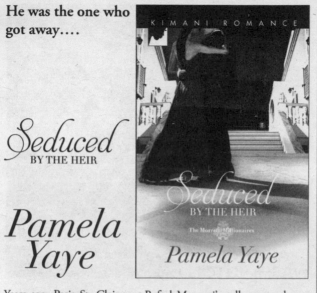
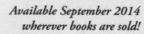